DEATH BY THE NUMBERS

There were three men facing Fargo at the poker table. And a packed saloon behind him. Starting something here would be like drawing to deuces against a full house.

But the Trailsman had an ace in the hole. His gun pointing under the table at the gang leader's belly.

"Somebody help me," the man called out. Fargo cursed as he heard movement behind him. If he turned, the trio in front of him would pour bullets into him.

With a heave, he lifted the table and sent it crashing into the man. Skye stayed low as he went with it, half turning to fire at a balding man whose Colt had cleared leather.

The man's breastbone vanished in an explosion of red. "That's one," Fargo murmured, and whipped his gun around . . . .

THE
TRAILSMAN
116

KANSAS
KILL

by

Jon Sharpe

A SIGNET BOOK

NEW AMERICAN LIBRARY

A DIVISION OF PENGUIN BOOKS USA INC., NEW YORK

Signet
Published by the Penguin Group
Penguin Books USA Inc., 375 Hudson Street,
New York, New York, 10014, U.S.A.
Penguin Books Ltd, 27 Wrights Lane, London W8 5TZ, England
Penguin Books Australia Ltd, Ringwood, Victoria, Australia
Penguin Books Canada Ltd, 2801 John Street,
Markham, Ontario, Canada L3R 1B4
Penguin Books (N.Z.) Ltd, 182-190 Wairau Road,
Auckland 10, New Zealand

Penguin Books Ltd, Registered Offices:
Harmondsworth, Middlesex, England

First published by Signet, an imprint of New American Library,
a division of Penguin Books USA Inc.

First Printing, August, 1991

10 9 8 7 6 5 4 3 2

The first chapter in this book previously appeared in *Gold Mine Madness*,
the one hundred and fifteenth volume in this series.

 REGISTERED TRADEMARK—MARCA REGISTRADA

Printed in Canada

BOOKS ARE AVAILABLE AT QUANTITY DISCOUNTS WHEN USED TO PROMOTE
PRODUCTS OR SERVICES. FOR INFORMATION PLEASE WRITE TO PREMIUM
MARKETING DIVISION, PENGUIN BOOKS USA INC., 375 HUDSON STREET,
NEW YORK, NEW YORK 10014.

The Trailsman

Beginnings . . . they bend the tree and they mark the man. Skye Fargo was born when he was eighteen. Terror was his midwife, vengeance his first cry. Killing spawned Skye Fargo; ruthless, cold-blooded murder. Out of the acrid smoke of gunpowder still hanging in the air, he rose, cried out a promise never forgotten.

The Trailsman they began to call him all across the West: searcher, scout hunter, the man who could see where others only looked, his skills for hire but not his soul, the man who lived each day to the fullest, yet trailed each tomorrow. Skye Fargo, the Trailsman, the seeker who could take the wildness of a land and the wanting of a woman and make them his own.

The Kansas Territory, 1861
where the Smokey Hills cast a long shadow
and human greed an even longer one . . .

1

He wasn't afraid. But he was nervous. There was no question about that, Doc Schubert admitted as he dried his freshly scrubbed hands and slipped into the long white laboratory gown. He tied the gown around his long, lanky figure and drew a deep breath. He hadn't done this kind of operation in years. In Clay Springs it was mostly broken bones and bullet wounds. Lottie. his nurse and companion for fifteen years, had just given the last dose of chloroform to the man stretched out on the operating table. Tom Johnson was not only one of the wealthiest ranchers in the region but an old friend, and Doc Schubert was determined to do the best his skills would let him.

Lottie waited, ready with cotton swabs, instruments, and bandages. Doc Schubert paused beside the table to glance at Alicia Johnson, clad in the white medical gown. Tom Johnson's wife, and some thirty years his junior, Alicia had insisted on being there. "You never know when you'll need an extra hand," she had said, and everyone knew how devoted she was to Tom. So he had agreed and given Alicia an afternoon of intensive instruction. She nodded to him now, standing back a few feet beside the table of extra bandages and extra basins of water. Doc Schubert returned the nod, paused beside the prostrate figure on the table, and picked up the scalpel from the instrument tray. He drew a deep breath and leaned forward.

His hand was steady, a reassuring feeling, as he made the first incision down Tom Johnson's belly. He felt Alicia Johnson flinch, cast a quick stare at her, and saw that she was all right and under control. Lottie reached forward with a clamp and sponges as he widened the incision. He worked quickly, pleased to feel the old deftness returning. Doc Schubert smiled. It was going well. He was just about to begin the critical phase of the operation when he heard the front door burst open. He whirled to stare at three men who rushed into the house, all with drawn guns.

"Get out of here," he shouted. "I'm in the middle of an operation." But the three men strode forward, the tallest one in front. "I've no money here. Get out," Doc Schubert shouted again. The tallest man brushed past him to halt beside the operating table. He fired three shots and Tom Johnson's opened, helpless body jerked convulsively as the bullets slammed into it. "Jesus," Doc Schubert swore as he dived forward and grabbed the man around the waist. But as he did, he heard the others open fire. He saw Lottie's white become red as bullets tore into her just before he felt the exploding, searing pain in his back as two shots struck him.

The man tore from his grasp as he fell forward and Doc Schubert felt the pain consuming him, welling up through his body, engulfing all else. He fell to one knee and, in his last moments of consciousness, he saw Alicia Johnson turn to flee when another shot rang out and she went down. Doc Schubert, his face contorted with excruciating pain, managed to gasp out a single word as the tall man stood over him. "Why?" he rasped, and pitched forward to the floor. His long, lanky body shuddered out its last breath and lay still.

The lights were burning brightly in the distant house, the big man noted as he rode slowly through the first lavender touch of twilight. Sitting casually astride the magnificent Ovaro with its glistening black fore and hind-quarters and gleaming pure-white midsection, the big man thought of how many years it had been since he last saw Doc Schubert. Skye Fargo smiled as the warm remembrance flowed through him. He and Doc had combined their efforts to bring in a wagon train riddled with sickness and Cheyenne arrows. It had been weeks of sweat, hard work and death waiting at every turn, the kind of effort that brings men together in a special bond.

When it was over, he'd seen Doc safely back to Clay Springs and stayed on himself for a spell. And now, with too many years in between, he'd finished a job near enough to Clay Springs for a surprise visit to Doc. He'd passed through town and he still had a few hundred yards to go when he saw the three men rush from the house and vault onto waiting horses. Fargo felt that frown dig into his brow as the three men raced away. Something more than apprehension instantly stabbed into him and he put the pinto into a gallop. The three riders were almost out of sight in the gathering dusk as they raced across the almost treeless flat land. He reached the house and skidded to a halt. Maybe Doc had sent the trio racing off on a mission, perhaps to bring back some special serum, Fargo murmured as he leapt to the ground. But the stabbing apprehension inside him told him that the thought was more hope than probability. He strode through the half-opened door, one hand on the butt of the big Colt at his hip.

Only silence greeted him as he stepped through the vestibule and into the next room, where he felt an oath stick in his throat. "God almighty," he breathed, his eyes sweeping the terrible scene spread out in front of him. Blood poured from the body on the operating table, not only from the incision opened in his abdomen but the three gaping bullet holes in his chest. Fargo's eyes went to the floor, where Doc Schubert lay in a widening circle of blood. He knelt down, pressed his fingers into Doc's neck to feel for a pulse. There was none and he cursed silently as he lifted his gaze. Lottie, Doc's nurse, lay at the head of the operating table in a lab coat that had once been white but was now almost entirely red.

He rose, stared down at the carnage, his lake-blue eyes narrowed as they took in every detail. He was about to leave when he heard the soft moan. The sound came from the adjoining room and he rushed in on one long stride to see the woman on the floor, one hand holding the back of her calf. She stared at him with brown, wide eyes that were a combination of hope and fear. "Jesus, you're alive," Fargo said, as he dropped to one knee beside her.

"Yes." She nodded. "I went down and they thought they'd killed me like they did the others."

Fargo moved her hand and saw the thin line of red running down a nicely turned calf. "The bullet passed through the fleshy part of your leg, but you'll still need it treated," he said, and paused to take in the woman. Between thirty and thirty-five, he guessed, a face a shade heavy but still very attractive, brown eyes that appraised with the look of someone who had seen

12

enough of the world, brown hair with a hint of red in it, and full lips on a wide mouth. A face that just avoided hardness, he decided. "What happened here?" he asked.

"Three men, looking to rob Doc Schubert, I guess. They just came in and started shooting," she said.

"What were you doing here?" Fargo questioned.

"I'm Alicia Johnson. The man on the operating table was my husband," she said.

"Jesus, I'm sorry," Fargo murmured, and rose to his feet, reached out, and lifted the woman onto a blue settee. "You'll be more comfortable on this," he said.

"There's a young doctor in Hillsdale, about five miles east. Maybe you could fetch him. I don't think I could ride," Alicia Johnson said. "Who are you, mister?" she asked.

"Fargo . . . Skye Fargo. I'm an old friend of Doc Schubert's. I came ready to pay him a surprise visit," Fargo said, and heard the bitter anger come into his voice.

"Skye Fargo? The one they call the Trailsman?" Alicia Johnson asked, and he nodded. "Tom and Doc Schubert were good friends and I've heard Doc talk about you."

"If I'd been five minutes earlier, this wouldn't have happened," Fargo bit out. "You've a sheriff in Clay Springs?"

"No, but Jack Hook is the undertaker and unofficial mayor. Get hold of him," Alicia Johnson said.

"I'll fetch the doc for you first," Fargo said.

"Yes, please," she said.

"Then I'm going to track down those three murdering bastards," Fargo said, his voice hardening.

Alicia Johnson's brown eyes stayed on him. "Maybe

13

I can help you with that," she said. "We'll talk after you get back."

Fargo nodded, spun on his heel, and strode into the adjoining room and past the scene of vicious death. Besides, he had already taken note of everything he needed to see.

Night had fallen when he rode the Ovaro east at a fast trot, letting the horse's powerful stride devour the relatively flat terrain. Not far away, the Smokey Hills rose up in rolling outline under a half-moon. He finally reached the town of Hillsdale, which turned out to be small, most of it warehouses and shops with but a few houses. He found someone who directed him to Doc Dawson's house, where he found a young man who was visibly shaken at what he heard.

"My God, Doc Schubert. He's been a real good friend since I came out here," the young man said, his voice quavering. "I'll get my rig. That way I can drive Alicia home."

"Good," Fargo said, and watched the younger man hurry to a small barn behind the house to reappear soon after driving a doctor's buggy with the high, overhanging roof and canework on the lower portion of the body. Fargo fell in beside him.

"Did you know Tom Johnson, too?" Doc Dawson asked as they moved through the night.

"No, just Doc Schubert," Fargo replied.

"Tom Johnson was well-liked and one of the richest ranchers in the region," the younger man said.

"From my quick look at him on the operating table I'd say he was pushing sixty," Fargo commented.

"Maybe a little more," Doc Dawson said. "He married Alicia five years ago, after his first wife, Vera, died. God, Alicia's lucky to be alive."

"Damn lucky," Fargo said. "But they won't get away with it."

"Hell, I'd say they have already. They're gone. God knows where," Doc Dawson said.

"They left a trail. Come morning, I'll pick it up. I'll get them," Fargo said, and his voice was a grim promise. The big, old house finally came into sight, lights burning brightly. As they reached it, Fargo saw a lone horse tethered outside. He held up one hand as he slid from the saddle. "Stay behind me," he said as the younger man swung from the wagon. Fargo entered the house with the Colt in hand, raised and ready to fire. He moved through the terrible scene and into the adjoining room. Alicia Johnson was still on the settee, her one leg resting stretched out, but she had company. A young woman turned as he entered and he saw the tearstains still on high cheekbones.

"It's him, the man I told you came in," Fargo heard Alicia say, and the young woman's face relaxed. Fargo saw Doc Dawson hurry past him, his little black bag in one hand, and go to Alicia.

"I'm Ellen Johnson," the young woman said, words coming with an effort. "I came by to see how Dad's operation had gone and found . . ." she said, her voice trailing off as she turned away. Fargo waited as she composed herself, and watched the doctor treat Alicia Johnson's calf wound. Ellen Johnson turned back to him and he took in an attractive face, perhaps a little long, with a straight nose, thin but nicely shaped lips. He saw light-blue eyes and very black hair cut short with long, very black narrow eyebrows to match. A long neck moved down to a narrow figure with breasts that flowed in a long, curving line under a white shirt. He guessed Ellen Johnson to be in her early twenties. "You were

15

coming to visit Doc Schubert, Alicia told me," she said.

"That's right, and I'm going to get the stinking bastards who did this," Fargo said. A quick glance at Alicia Johnson saw that the doc had her calf tightly bandaged and was helping her to stand.

"You'll be able to walk fine in a day or two, but keep the bandage on till I come see you," Doc Dawson told Alicia. The woman had taken off the long white laboratory coat and Fargo saw a full figure, perhaps ten pounds too much on it, but she carried it well. Her breasts had no sag in them, her wide hips and strong full thighs pressed against a black skirt. There was a ripe sensuousness to Alicia Johnson, he decided.

"You had something to tell me," Fargo reminded the woman.

"Yes. I know where they were going," she said. Fargo felt his brows lift in surprise. "To Rock Station," Alicia Johnson said. "One of them, the tall one, said so. He has a sandy mustache and a scar on his lower lip."

"How'd he come to say so?" Fargo questioned.

"I heard him tell the others they'd meet there. I guess they intended to separate," Alicia said.

"That's smart thinking on their part," Doc Dawson put in, and Fargo nodded agreement. "I'll take Alicia back to the ranch now," the doctor said.

Fargo glanced at Ellen Johnson. "You go with them. There's nothing you can do here except take in more pain," he said.

"I don't live at the ranch. I've my own place," Ellen Johnson said, a flash of pointedness in her tone.

"I'll see you home," Fargo said.

"Thanks, but I'll be all right. You go on. Getting those murdering killers comes first," she said.

"Rock Station's a full day's ride. I've plenty of time. I'll see you back," Fargo said.

The young woman drew a deep sigh. "All right. I'd really appreciate that. I'm feeling pretty shaky," she said. She walked through the other room with her eyes staring straight ahead and Fargo followed but hung back a moment to sweep the terrible scene again with a quick but penetrating glance. His mouth was a thin line when he strode outside. Alicia was in the doctor's buggy as he paused. Her brown eyes sought him out.

"You'll come back and tell me, won't you? I won't be sleeping much till I know they've paid for this," she said.

"Count on it," Fargo said, and Alicia let gratefulness pass through her full-cheeked face. Doc Dawson rolled the buggy forward and Fargo climbed onto the Ovaro and swung alongside Ellen Johnson's light bay. He rode beside her as she followed the buggy for some quarter-mile and then cut west from the road. He rode in silence with her and heard her struggle with sobs until she finally gained back at least surface composure. "You were close to your pa," he remarked softly.

"Very," Ellen Johnson said.

"How long since you moved from your pa's ranch?" Fargo asked.

"Since Alicia moved in," Ellen said, fell silent for a moment, and threw him a sharp, sidelong glance. "And I know what you're thinking," she said.

"And what would that be?" he asked.

"Daughter resents new wife," she snapped.

"It happens often enough."

"I suppose it does."

"Then sometimes people just don't get along together," Fargo said.

17

"And sometimes there's a lot more," Ellen said as she led him through a line of silver maple to a modest ranch house with three corrals and a barn spread out behind it. "Home, sweet home," she said, and dismounted in front of the house. "Thanks for seeing me back."

"My pleasure," Fargo said.

"I'd invite you in, but I know you want to get on your way and I don't feel much like playing hostess," Ellen said. There was a direct frankness to her, very likable in its own way, he decided. "You told Alicia you'd be back to tell her you settled accounts. Would it be too much to ask you to stop by here?"

"I planned to do that, especially as how there's something strange about this whole thing," Fargo said.

"Something strange?" Ellen Johnson frowned. "Because it was so vicious?"

"It was that, but I've seen vicious before. There was something else."

The young woman's frown deepened. "Such as?" she pressed.

"I don't know, not yet. Maybe I'll have some answers when I get back," Fargo said.

"Be careful. I wouldn't want to see you as their fourth victim," Ellen Johnson said.

"Me neither," Fargo said with a wry grin as he wheeled the horse around. He left her frowning after him, a slender, lovely figure that combined pain and lonely strength.

He put the pinto into a steady trot northeast, his thoughts already turned to the task ahead. An apparent random robbery attempt that turned into three vicious murders. Only maybe there had been nothing random at all. There had been little things. He had picked them up. His Trailsman's eye always searched for the little things. Sometimes they were unimportant. Sometimes they meant everything. He was going to find out about these. Doc Schubert deserved that.

2

He rode until the moon was in the midnight sky before pulling up for the night. It had been a long day, and tomorrow would be longer. He didn't intend to be exhausted when he faced three ruthless killers. He slept quickly, and when morning came, he was riding on at a steady pace that brought him to his destination a few hours after dark. Station Rock wasn't much of a town, existing mainly as a stop for the Kansas-Nebraska Stage. There wasn't even a boardinghouse, Fargo noted as he rode slowly along the main street. That actually made his task easier, he realized. It left only one place for him to look. He drew to a halt in front of the saloon.

In a town such as Station Rock, the saloon was more than a saloon. It was the place that drew the kind of men he sought as a magnet draws steel filings. He dropped the Ovaro's reins over the hitching post and walked into the smoky room. A long bar took up one wall, a small clear space on the floor in front of it. The rest of the room was filled with tables, most of them harboring cardplayers or serious drinkers.

Fargo paused at the bar to let his gaze travel slowly across the room as he scanned those gathered at each table. He halted at a round table a few feet from the rear door of the room. Three men played blackjack at the table and Fargo's eyes narrowed on the tall one. Alicia Johnson's description had been excellent, he noted as he took in the man's sand-colored mustache and scarred lower lip. Fargo glanced at the other two men, one with straight black hair that hung in thick strands, the other balding with a heavy-lipped face.

The tall one kept a tan stetson on as he played, and Fargo's thoughts raced through his mind. There were three of them and none objected to cold-blooded killing. He had to get some advantage, even a small one, and he considered waiting till they left the saloon. He quickly discarded the thought. They'd be afoot with more room to maneuver, and he'd be at more of a disadvantage. But he didn't want a shoot-out with innocent bystanders killed while they played cards. Besides, he wanted some answers from them. He let his thoughts turn a few moments more and then began to stroll toward the table. One thing he had decided: if it came to a sudden shoot-out, the tall one would go first. He was the leader, the strongest of the trio. The other two would be quicker to talk.

He came to the table and halted beside an empty chair. "Mind if I sit in?" He smiled.

"It's a private game," the mustached one growled, not bothering to look up from his cards. Fargo half-shrugged as he sat down and pulled the chair close to the table. The man looked up, this time. "You deaf, mister?" he said, frowning.

"No, I hear fine. But I don't listen well," Fargo said, still smiling. The man stared at him but behind the stare Fargo saw the moment of apprehensive perplexity. "Besides, I like to ask questions," Fargo said and caught the uneasy glances the other two men exchanged.

"You some kind of goddamn fool?" The tall one

frowned. "Get the hell away from here before I put a bullet between your eyes."

"Soon as you tell me about Doc Schubert," Fargo said calmly.

The other man's face froze for an instant. "I don't know any Doc Schubert," he said.

"Sure you do. You killed him and two other people back at Clay Springs," Fargo said. He kept his arm motionless as, under the table, he used his hand and wrist to slide the Colt from its holster.

"You're crazy, mister," the man rasped. "And I'm gonna kill you for that."

"Maybe, but right now there's a big old Colt pointed right at your belly," Fargo said, and the man's eyes widened for an instant.

"There are three of us. One of us will get you," the man growled.

"I expect so, but not before I blow away your belly," Fargo said calmly. "Your call."

The man's lips drew so tight that his scar almost disappeared. "Who the hell are you, mister?" he asked through unmoving lips.

"A friend of Doc Schubert. Now, we're going to take a little walk outside," Fargo said, and flicked a glance at the other two. "You follow and he's a dead man," Fargo said, and returned his eyes to the mustached one. The man's thoughts were racing, mirrored in his furious glare as he sought options. Fargo's eyes, ice-blue, bored into the man. "Get up real slow or get dead real fast," Fargo said. "What's your call?"

The man delayed another thirty seconds before turning unexpectedly clever, lifting his voice in a sudden shout. "Somebody help me. This bastard's going to gun me down," he called out. Fargo heard the murmur of voices come to a stop behind him and he cursed in silence at the man's cunning. If he turned to address the others, the trio would be up and shooting instantly. If he fired the Colt there was no way of telling what the crowd might do. "Somebody help me. He's got a gun on me now," Fargo heard the man call out. "Don't let him gun me down in cold blood."

Fargo cursed again silently as he heard the movement behind him, voices rising. The trio waited for him to turn to the crowd. They'd need only a split second to pour bullets into him. "Son of a bitch," he muttered as he saw the gleam of anticipation in the mustached one's eyes. Gathering his arm and shoulder muscles, both his forearms still under the table, he lifted and upended the table, sending it crashing into the man as it knocked him into the wall. He stayed low as he went with it, driving it backward with its shoulder to pin the man against the wall.

He half-turned at the same time and fired at the balding man who had gotten his gun out of its holster and saw the man's breastbone vanish in an explosion of red. "That's one, Doc," Fargo murmured as he dived and rolled as the second man fired. The crowd had halted in confusion and fear, some diving for safety, others falling back. Fargo heard the bullet whistle past his head from the rear as the mustached figure pushed himself out from behind the table and fired. Fargo dived and rolled as two more bullets smashed into the floor. He threw himself forward, slammed into the rear door with his shoulder, and fell into the dark outside. He came up on one knee, the Colt raised and aimed at the half-open rear door.

But no one came out and, with an oath, he leapt to his feet and raced for the front door of the saloon. He rounded the corner of the building to see the black-haired figure climbing onto his horse, the mustached one already in the saddle and racing away. Fargo halted, aimed, and the Colt barked once. The man's thick black hair flew almost horizontally from his head as the bullet plowed into the back of his head. He pitched forward before toppling from the horse. "That's two, Doc," Fargo hissed, reloading as he ran. He reached the Ovaro and leapt into the saddle, wheeled the horse, and took after the fleeing figure, who had already left town. Fargo caught a glimpse of the racing horse moving up into tree-covered hillside terrain.

He swerved the pinto to take a distance-cutting angle up the hillside and a half-moon let him glimpse the fleeing rider move into a stand of black walnut. He saw the man cast a glance backward and use his reins to whip the horse forward. But the trees formed their own obstacle course and he made little time as he had to swerve his way forward.

The Ovaro's powerful hindquarters gave Fargo an extra manueverability and the horse seemed to delight in the challenge as he skirted, darted, and spun his way through the wooded terrain. The fleeing rider was plainly in sight now and Fargo flattened himself as he saw the man half-turn in the saddle and fire two shots at him. The man swerved to his left, slowed, and fired two more shots, both wide of their mark. Fargo brought the pinto in closer and suddenly the man reined to a halt, took the time to aim, and Fargo flattened against the side of the Ovaro's powerful neck as the two bullets whizzed just past his head.

He lifted himself up, yanked the Colt out, and saw the man start to send his horse forward again. "Hold it there or you're dead," Fargo shouted, and saw the man rein up, come to a halt, and stand quietly. Fargo moved foward, lowered the Colt. Suddenly the man flung himself sideways from the horse. "Damn," Fargo swore as he saw the figure land in the tall brush. Fargo moved a few paces closer and leapt to the ground, his eyes sweeping the brush for any sign of movement, the Colt poised and ready to fire. He took a half-dozen steps forward, heard the sound of brush rustling, and halted, listening. The brush rustled again, but the man wasn't crawling, the sound was too stationary for that. He was reloading. Fargo cursed as he threw himself sideways behind the wide trunk of an old walnut as a hail of bullets erupted.

Fargo stayed crouched behind the trunk, counting as he heard most of the bullets slam into the bark of the tree. When the sixth bullet landed, he was on his feet and racing around the tree to where the brush had rustled. He halted, the Colt aimed. "Out, goddamn you," he barked. His only answer was absolute silence. His quarry was neither crawling nor reloading. He'd hear either, Fargo knew. The man was playing possum, hoping his pursuer would move in the wrong direction and give him time to reload. Fargo cursed silently. He still wanted the man alive. He aimed the Colt at the top area of the brush, fired, then bracketed the area with two more shots lower down at each side. He moved in closer to the center and fired again and paused to reload. The man could see him through the brush, he knew as he raised the gun again and fired off two more bracketing shots, close to the center of the area.

"All right," the man called out. "I'm comin' out."

Fargo stepped back a pace, kept the Colt aimed, and saw the figure lift itself from the tall brush.

"This way, nice and slow," Fargo said. The man

advanced, his arms hanging loosely. As he stepped from the brush, Fargo saw that he held his gun in one hand. "Drop it right there," Fargo said, and the man let the gun slide from his grasp. He took three steps forward and sank down to the ground as Fargo stared at him. He lay motionless in a crumpled heap and Fargo moved toward him, a frown creasing his brow. Had one of his shots hit the man? he wondered. He reached the crumpled form, bent over the figure when the man erupted and Fargo glimpsed the moonlight glint on a knife blade as it swept up at him in a short arc.

He twisted backward, off-balance, and felt the blade graze his chin. He continued to fall away and saw the man leap at him, the knife raised again to strike. Fargo dived and heard the knife hiss past his back as he hit the ground, rolled, and came up on his knees. The man charged again, knife raised. Fargo managed to bring the Colt up and he fired, the range almost point-blank. He saw the man quiver but the charging figure's momentum was too much to halt. Fargo flung himself sideways as the man's body hurtled over him to land facedown against the base of a tree.

Fargo rose, stepped to the figure, the Colt aimed downward as he used his foot to turn the body over. The man stared up at him with unseeing eyes, his sand-colored mustache red with the blood that flowed from his open mouth. Fargo swore silently, turned and strode to the Ovaro. "That's three, Doc," he said grimly as he swung into the saddle and rode away. He kept riding till the moon was nearly across the far reaches of the night sky before he halted and slept into the morning sun.

When he woke, he washed at a stream and rode south toward Clay Springs. Ellen Johnson's place was on the way and it was late afternoon when he reached the modest ranch. She ran from the house as she saw him ride up, looking lovely as a wild columbine in a red blouse and dark-green skirt. "Thought I'd pick you up on the way to Alicia's," Fargo said. "No sense in telling things twice."

"I'll get my horse," she said, and ran to the barn. Fargo watched a half-dozen young quarter horses romp in one of the corrals until she reappeared on the light bay. 'I'm glad to see you back in one piece," Ellen Johnson said as she swung in beside him.

"That makes two of us," he returned.

She cast a sidelong glance at him and the question hung in her eyes. "Did you find them?" she asked "You can tell me that much now."

"I found them," he said grimly. "They're dead."

She rode in silence for a long moment. "I thought I'd feel more," she said finally. "Happiness, satisfaction, triumph. But I don't. Not yet, anyway."

"You will."

"Yes, but somehow it seems wrong to feel those things over more killing," Ellen Johnson said, and cast another glance at his chiseled jaw. "I take it you don't agree with that."

"That's right. I'm an Old Testament man. An eye for an eye," he said. "Specially when it comes to vermin."

She took in his answer and was silent and he let her lead the way to the Johnson ranch, which turned out to be an imposing spread nestled in a dip in the land. A big ranch house formed the centerpiece, flanked by barns, bunkhouses, and large cattle corrals, all neatly painted and in top condition. Everything was flanked by shade trees, mostly box elder and shagbark hickory.

He rode up to the main house with Ellen. They dismounted as an elderly man not over five feet four inches tall and wearing a white butler's jacket opened the front door of the house.

"Hello, Miss Ellen," he said deferentially.

"Hello, George," Ellen said.

"Mrs. Townsend is waiting in the drawing room," the man said.

"Let's go see Mrs. Townsend," Ellen said to Fargo with sarcastic heaviness on the last two words. Fargo followed her into a large and richly furnished room with deep leather chairs and a wide sofa, tapestries on the walls, and thick carpet underfoot.

Alicia Johnson turned as they entered, a royal-blue dress outlining the fullness of her deep-breasted figure, a low-cut neckline revealing both edges of two round, cream-white mounds. Her eyes searched Fargo's face as she came forward.

"It's done," he said quietly.

Her brown eyes continued to search his. "You killed all three of them," Alicia murmured, and he nodded.

"Not exactly the way I wanted, but it's done," Fargo said.

Alicia Johnson's arms went around his neck as she held him for a long moment, the scent of her perfume dark and sensual. He felt the pillowy softness of her breasts against his chest. "Thank you. Oh, dear, wonderful man, thank you," Alicia murmured. She pulled back and dropped her arms from around his neck, but her hands clung to his. He saw Ellen looking up, her face expressionless and yet, somehow, disdainful. "We'll be burying Tom in the morning, along with Doc Schubert and poor Lottie," Alicia said. "Knowing those killers paid for what they did will help the hurting."

"I hope so," Fargo said.

"Fargo's got something to say," Ellen's voice cut in brusquely, and she received a frown from Alicia.

Fargo smiled. "Fargo can talk for himself, honey," he said to Ellen. The gentle reprimand drew only a flare from her light-blue eyes.

"Then talk," she snapped. "You hinted at things that've kept me from sleeping ever since."

Fargo brought his eyes back to Alicia. "I told Ellen there was something strange about the killings," he said. "I still think so."

"Strange?" Alicia frowned. "Three killers come in to rob Doc Schubert and kill everyone else so there are no witnesses left to talk. Or think they did. It's horrible but what's strange about it?"

"I don't think they came to rob Doc Schubert's office. That's how it was supposed to look, but I don't think that's what it was," Fargo said. Alicia's frown stayed and now Ellen stared at him with her lips parted.

"What are you saying?" Alicia asked.

"I'm saying they didn't come to rob Doc Schubert. They came to kill Tom Johnson," Fargo said, and heard Ellen's gasp of shock.

"How can you come to that conclusion?" Alicia asked.

"First, you come to rob somebody, he's your chief target. These three stepped past Doc Schubert and poured three shots into Tom Johnson on the operating table. He was the one they wanted to make sure was dead. He was their real target. They gunned down everyone else afterward," Fargo said. "Second, they didn't stay to look for any money. Nothing was disturbed, not even a desk drawer opened. They didn't even go through Doc Schubert's pockets. They killed and ran.''

''They probably heard you coming and decided to run,'' Alicia offered.

Fargo shook his head. ''I was too far away for them to hear me,'' he said.

''My God. They came to kill Daddy,'' Ellen breathed, her voice made of shock.

Alicia turned to the younger woman. ''Don't go off half-cocked,'' she snapped sternly. ''Fargo has put together conclusions. They're hardly facts.''

''That's true,'' Fargo agreed. ''But they hold together for me.''

''Me, too,'' Ellen said.

Alicia Johnson's brown eyes returned to Fargo. ''If someone wanted Tom killed, why would they do it that way?'' she asked.

''It was a perfect time and place. He was a helpless target and robbery a perfect cover,'' Fargo answered.

Alicia considered the reply, her face wreathed in thought. ''I suppose it's possible,'' she murmured. ''But we'll never know now that the three killers are dead.''

''I'll find out if it's so,'' Ellen cut in. ''There's got to be a way, even with them dead.'' She turned to Fargo, plea for help in her eyes.

''Maybe and then maybe not,'' he told her. ''But there's a place to start.''

''Where?'' Ellen asked.

''Who had a reason to want your pa dead? Another rancher? Someone he feuded with? Somebody from the past? Old enemies come back?'' Fargo said.

''I don't know anyone who's come back.'' Ellen frowned into space. ''I'll have to think about this.''

31

Alicia's voice cut in. "If you're bent on pursuing this, I can think of someone," she said. "Royd Haggard. He's always hated your father."

"Royd?" Ellen echoed, uncertainty in her voice.

"He's a rancher in the area," Alicia explained to Fargo. "He was furious when Tom cornered the cattle sale at Abilene. He threatened Tom then, but Tom dismissed it as just talk."

"Maybe it was more than talk," Ellen put in.

"Even so, you can't go around accusing someone on Fargo's conclusions," Alicia warned.

"No, you can't," Fargo agreed.

"What about Amos? I'm sure he could be of help," Ellen said, a burst of excitement coloring her voice.

"That shiftless old fool? Nonsense," Alicia snapped.

"Daddy and Amos had a special relationship all their lives," Ellen said defensively.

"Tom indulged the old fool. Amos Dillon was some kind of project for him, one I could never understand," Alicia said.

"You never could and never tried," Ellen said, ice on each word. "Amos wasn't a project. They were friends. They had a special kind of friendship."

"Don't criticize me. You never understood it, either. Nobody did," Alicia flared.

"I never dismissed it. I never belittled it and I won't now," Ellen said, hurt in her voice, and she spun on her heel to pause at the door. "I'll be thinking about what you've said, Fargo. Stop by. I'll have things to tell you."

"All right."

"Will you stay for supper, Fargo?" Alicia asked. "I've something to discuss with you."

"My pleasure. I never turn down a good meal or a warm woman," Fargo said.

"Now you'll have two for the price of one," Ellen flung back as she stormed from the house.

Alicia's eyes stayed on the empty doorway for a moment, her lips drawn in. "She's always been difficult. She's impossible now that she's so upset. I wouldn't pay too much mind to anything she says," Alicia said.

The elderly little manservant appeared in the doorway to an adjoining room. "Supper's ready, Mrs. Johnson," he said.

Fargo felt Alicia's arm slide into his as she walked into the dining room with him. He saw a table beautifully set with a white lace tablecloth, fine china, and gleaming crystal. Alicia took her place at the head of the table and had him sit to her right as the servant poured wine into fine goblets.

"To tomorrow," Alicia said, lifting her glass in a toast.

Fargo raised his glass in a reply, a little surprised that the toast hadn't been to the memory of Tom Johnson. He gave his own silent toast to Doc Schubert and felt the warm, rich liquid flow down his throat. "I'm no wine expert, but I know something special when I taste it," he commented.

"Chambertin, 1847," Alicia said. She sat back and her brown eyes surveyed the big man beside her. Fargo, in turn, found himself admiring a highly attractive woman to whom the wine imparted an added glow as her cheeks turned a faint pink. She leaned forward and her hand came over his on the table. "I can't tell you how much I appreciate what you've done. You've brought some measure to justice for Tom, Doc Schubert, and poor Lottie,'' Alicia said.

"Real justice means getting at the real truth," Fargo said.

"Of course, but if that's impossible, we must settle for what we have," Alicia said.

"That's so, only I don't think Ellen's in a mood for much settling," Fargo pointed out as the meal was served. They ate a good hen boiled with stock, herbs, and spices. It was absolutely delicious.

"She'll settle down when she realizes there's nothing to be found," Alicia said. "I still think it was a simple robbery that perhaps went wrong."

"What about this Amos person?" Fargo asked.

"An old recluse who lives in the Smokey Hills. For some reason I could never understand, Tom paid regular visits to him, kept him supplied with food and whiskey," Alicia said with a trace of disdain in her voice.

"You ever meet him?"

"God, no, and I've no desire to," Alicia said. "He can stay a recluse and wither away for all I care. I've more important things to tend to. With Tom gone, the ranch is my responsibility. That's why I asked you to stay." Fargo's brows arched at the remark and she gave him a warm smile. "I've a job for you. Tom wanted to see if there was a way to drive cattle through the Smokey Hills. That'd save two weeks of driving a herd west and then north. I want you to see if you can find one. Your usual fee, whatever it is, more if you want."

"The usual will be fine," Fargo said.

"Wonderful. I really need to know whether it's possible or whether to forget about it. Time's important," Alicia said.

"I'll start tomorrow, after the funeral," Fargo said, and Alicia's hand found his again with a warm squeeze.

"Thank you," she murmured.

"Thanks for the mighty fine meal," he returned. "I'm glad I stayed."

"That's good. I don't like eating alone," Alicia said as he finished the last of his wine and rose to his feet. "You're welcome to stay the night. There's plenty of room," she said.

"Maybe some other time," he said, and found her arm linked into his as he started for the door.

"Oh, yes, you promised Ellen you'd visit," she said.

"I did," he said.

"Just remember, she's a very upset young woman," Alicia said as they reached the door. She drew her arm from his and suddenly her lips were brushing his cheek, softly moist, lingering for a moment and then drawing away. "Good night, Fargo," she said, and left him with an enigmatic little smile as she closed the door. A very compelling woman, as attractive as she was controlled, he decided.

It was obvious that Alicia Johnson had a much firmer grip on everything than Ellen. But then she had a dozen years more of life behind her, and life teaches lessons. Yet that wasn't a complete answer, he admitted to himself as he rode through the night. He'd seen plenty come apart despite the years they had behind them. No, Alicia was a woman as strong as she was attractive, and she had probably always been that way.

He took a low hillside that brought him heading closer to Ellen's place, and he wondered if it was perhaps too late to visit. But the house was fully lighted when he came in sight of it. He rode to the front door at a slow walk. Ellen answered the door at his knock, still in the

35

red blouse, her light-blue eyes coolly appraising.

"I'd given you up," she commented.

"I said I'd stop by," Fargo reminded her.

Ellen Johnson shrugged. "People change plans given the right reasons. Or the wrong ones."

He stepped inside and fastened her with a speculative glance. "I'm wondering," he said.

"Wondering what?"

"If you've such a sharp tongue when you're not upset."

She blinked. "Some people bring it out of me."

"I'd say Alicia's more patient with your tongue than most would be," Fargo said.

"For instance?"

"That remark about two for the price of one. That seemed plain bitchy."

"It was plain true," Ellen sniffed. There was no concession in her, he saw. "You come to lecture or listen?" she tossed at him.

"Listen," he said.

She turned away to pause beside a small table, her breasts swaying in unison. She picked up a square of notepaper. "I've been going over people around Clay Springs, eliminating most everybody. Daddy was well-liked. I'll give you those I didn't cross off, starting with Alicia's suggestion, Royd Haggard. He's a hard, mean man with no scruples, that's true, and there's always been bad blood between him and my father. I've got to make him a suspect. Then there's Zach Traynor. Pa fired him a month ago for stealing at the ranch. He swore vengeance and he's a bitter, vengeful man. He certainly has to be included," Ellen said, and halted.

"That's all? Those two?" Fargo frowned.

She wrinkled up her face. "One more. Billy Harrison.

He was real sweet on me, wanted to marry me," she said.

"And you?" Fargo queried.

"I thought he was the greatest. I was real taken by him. He's handsome and smooth. But Daddy never liked him. He kept saying there was something wrong with Billy. Of course, that made me only see him more. And then Daddy came up with the truth about Billy. Seems Billy had killed three men and been in jail when he was only fifteen, down in New Mexico. He got out because he got some woman to lie for him. She admitted it later, after he was out and gone and had dumped her," Ellen said. "I saw that Daddy had been right about Billy all along by how mean and nasty Billy turned when the truth came out. He just up and shot a dog that got in his way one morning. I knew then I'd been a blind little fool."

"And you think this Billy Harrison would have your dad killed?" Fargo asked.

"Yes. He even said he would."

"You know where he is now?"

"He does hired cowhanding for different ranchers in the area. He's got a shack at the foot of Ridge Hill east of here," Ellen said.

"Anybody else?" Fargo questioned, and she shook her head. "Any past enemies?"

"Not that I know about. If there was, I'll bet Amos could tell us," Ellen said.

"Alicia feels Amos Dillon is a worthless old recluse," Fargo said.

"He's a recluse and a strange man, but Daddy and he have been friends for a lifetime. I can't see my father being friends with anyone who's worthless. There was some kind of real bond. My mother always accepted it. It was something Daddy had, and that was enough for her. Alicia, of course, couldn't stand to see him spend time or money on anyone or anything but her.''

"You ever meet Amos Dillon?'' Fargo queried.

"Over the years? Yes, at least a half-dozen times,'' Ellen said.

"Then you know where he lives in the hills.''

"No, nobody does. He hides away. Only Daddy could find him. We have to talk to Amos. I know Daddy visited with him only a few days before the operation. I'm sure Amos could help us,'' Ellen said.

"We'd have to find him first,'' Fargo said.

"You could do it. I'll hire you to find him, pay you whatever you want,'' Ellen said. "You're the Trailsman. I know you could find him.''

"Alicia's hired me to find a cattle trail through the Smokey Hills. I start tomorrow,'' Fargo said.

Ellen frowned at him. "Tell her you've something more important to do,'' she said.

"I made an agreement. I don't go back on my word,'' Fargo said.

"Dammit, Fargo, you raised this. You can't just turn your back on it now,'' Ellen said. He winced inwardly. She could spear with words.

"I raised questions. I didn't say I'd chase down answers, especially ones that might never be found,'' Fargo said.

"You want to believe killing Doc Schubert's murderers was enough. It wasn't, and you know it,'' she flung back, and he swore silently at her.

"All right, I'll help you when I get back,'' he conceded.

"No, tell Alicia to wait,'' Ellen snapped.

"I made an agreement. I told you, I don't break

agreements. You can wait till I get back. The answers to this won't go away," he told her.

"They might," she glowered.

"You can wait," he said, and turned from her. She walked to the door and watched him climb onto the pinto with the glower still on her face. "I'll be in touch," Fargo said as he put the pinto into a trot and rode into the night. He heard the door slam shut as he moved up a small rise. She'd wait, he told himself. She had no choice, really.

He found a spot to bed down on top of the rise and went to sleep aware that he wished he could feel more confident about Ellen Johnson.

3

The foot of the burying hill was crowded with wagons when Fargo reached the scene just outside of Clay Springs. Most were ranch wagons, buckboards, cut-under buggies, and slat-bottom road wagons, but he saw a goodly sprinkling of standing-top phaetons and round-bottom bretts. People of substance had come from good distances, it was obvious. The near-noon sun was hot as he dismounted and climbed to a spot at the edge of the crowd.

He spied Alicia, in black and a black veil, standing with a group of men who were obviously ranch hands and other employees. His eyes found Ellen to one side, standing among the other mourners yet looking very much alone, a black blouse and black skirt making her lean figure seem even leaner. Her fine-featured face showed the strain in the tightness of it. He saw her hands were tightly clenched at her sides.

The preacher began the service and his eulogies seemed geared to the importance of the deceased in the community, the longest reserved for Tom Johnson with Doc Schubert next, and only a few kind but brief words for Lottie, the nurse.

The preacher made the most of his moment in the limelight, and only when the three caskets were lowered

41

into the ground did Fargo step back. He stayed beneath a tree and watched the mourners leave until there was only one figure left at the gravesite. He waited until she finally turned and came down the hill. Now he saw the tears staining Ellen's cheeks.

She paused as he stepped forward and instantly read the question in his eyes. "None of them was here," she said, and walked on.

He let her go and saw Alicia riding away with another couple in the slat-bottom phaeton. He slowly scanned the surroundings for any sign of distant onlookers, but there were none and he walked to where he had left the Ovaro and climbed into the saddle.

The day had gone into the afternoon as he rode through town, this time taking the time to note the shops and stores that made up Clay Springs. Not a large town, it was neater than many, but the saloon and dance hall was the largest structure, sitting in the center of town. THE CLAY SPRINGS PLAYHOUSE, a large sign proclaimed over the swinging doors of the entranceway. He'd be giving the place a visit. There was no place better to pick up rumor that often held truth in it than the local saloon, and a triple killing would bring its share of talk in any town. The local saloon was an equally good place to spread rumor, and that might be in order, he mused as he rode on.

When he left the town, he headed north to the rolling high land of the Smokey Hills. The day had reached midafternoon when he began to climb into the hills and quickly found himself in terrain heavy with tree cover, mostly shagbark hickory, black walnut, and box elder with plenty of tall underbrush and long beds of wildflowers. He halted halfway into the hills to survey the land to his right and left and to chew on a stick of beef jerky from his saddlebag. He saw nothing along the southern expanse of hills that would let more than two steers through at a time, the land beautifully rolling but heavily overgrown and marked by successive hills and dips. But there were two other approaches up into the hills to explore, he reminded himself.

He had started to turn the horse east when his eyes caught the movement of tree leaves a hundred yards to his left. He immediately drew the Ovaro into a cluster of black walnut and his eyes peered at the distant spot as they traced the movement of the leaves. A rider moving through the trees, slowly, he told himself, the swaying branches marking the horseman's progress. Suddenly the rider came into view, a man wearing a black duster and moving slowly along the edge of a narrow ridge. He paused, moved on again, turned to his right, paused again. He was plainly watching something below where he rode, and Fargo turned the pinto up a slope but stayed in the trees.

He climbed up onto higher ground, turned and found a straight stretch of land that let him see the horseman below and the lower hills beyond. It took a few moments, but he found what the man watched. His jaw tightened as he caught the light bay with the straight-backed, slender figure stop it.

"Damn," he hissed. She had changed to a dark-green shirt, but there was no mistaking the black hair and the willowy figure. He watched Ellen slowly move through the hills, pause, take a gentle slope, halt at the top, pause again, and move down the other side. She was doing more than searching the lower hills, he realized. She was waiting to be seen, pausing at open places, turning slowly on a cleared ridge, staying in the clear as she rode up and down the slopes.

She was giving Amos Dillon a chance to see her. Maybe the man was indeed watching her from some hidden place in the hills. And perhaps he was hard asleep someplace. But someone was watching her every move. Fargo's glance went to the horseman in the black duster as the man continued to parallel Ellen's movements, never taking his eyes from her. Fargo kept pace as he watched the watcher. When the horseman began to move downhill, his eyes went to Ellen. She had broken off her wandering and headed down through the lower hills. Fargo saw the man increase speed and circle to one side, plainly bent on flanking Ellen. Fargo took the Ovaro downhill but stayed inside the trees as he moved after Ellen.

He was still some twenty yards away in the trees when he came level with her and saw the horse and rider charge out of the hickory on the other side. Ellen spun in surprise, but the man was at her in seconds. He flung one arm straight out and it caught Ellen across the collarbone. She flew from the horse and hit the ground on her back. Fargo saw the man leap from his horse, his long, black duster billowing out behind him as he landed almost on top of Ellen.

Fargo pulled the big Sharps from its saddle holster as he leapt from the Ovaro. When he hit the ground, he saw that the man had flung himself atop Ellen before she could get up. Ellen kicked out, a flash of long, lovely leg as she tried to get away, but he had her pinned down and Fargo heard his harsh laugh. "Enjoy it, baby, enjoy it. It might be your last lay," the man rasped, and pushed Ellen's legs farther apart as he pinned her arms down to the ground. Ellen's cry was made of pain and fury as her attacker pressed down over her, positioning himself for enjoyment as he ignored her flailing legs.

Fargo paused, dropped to one knee, and brought the rifle to his shoulder. He aimed, then swore silently as the big black duster enveloped both the man and Ellen so that a shot might hit the young woman. His lips pulled back in distaste, Fargo moved the rifle to his right as Ellen continued to struggle and the duster lifted and fell back and lifted again. Fargo took aim again and fired this time. The man shouted an oath of pain as the heavy rifle bullet shattered his calf bone. Ellen pushed herself backward along the ground as her attacker rolled off her, clutching at his leg as he swore in pain again.

Fargo ran from the trees, the rifle in one hand. The man lay almost hidden under the folds of the long, black duster, his one leg drawn up. Fargo ran toward him and suddenly the duster was pulled back and Fargo saw a six-gun in the man's hand as he lifted himself onto an elbow. Fargo flung himself into a sideways dive as the shot grazed his shoulder. He hit the ground and rolled. He let the rifle drop and yanked at his Colt as he kept rolling. The man shifted to fire again, but his movements were both painful and slow as he dragged his shattered calf. His shot went over Fargo's head with a few inches to spare. Fargo had the Colt out and he fired with no time to pinpoint shots. He saw the man's body jerk upward and back as the two shots slammed into him and then lay still. The long black duster settled itself over him with shroudlike appropriateness.

Fargo rose to his feet and saw Ellen stand, her light blue eyes wide as she watched him walk to the silent figure. She stayed frozen in place for a moment and then she was running forward, fell hard against Fargo's chest.

"Oh, God, thank you, thank you," she murmured, pulled back, and looked up at him with gratefulness filling her eyes. "I guess this is my lucky day, you being here at the right moment."

"I told you to wait till I got back," Fargo said, his face hard.

She stepped back and met the coldness of his eyes with instant defiance. "I never said I would," she snapped.

"My mistake. I didn't realize you were that dumb."

"I'm not dumb and this is further proof," she said, and gestured to the slain man.

"Proof of what?"

"That somebody didn't want me to talk to Amos Dillon."

"How many people did you tell you were going to go look for Amos?" Fargo questioned.

"I may have mentioned it to a few people before the service, but they were friends of Daddy's. They wouldn't try to stop me," Ellen said.

"Friends talk. Others overhear," Fargo said as he bent down and began to go through the man's pockets. He pulled a slip of paper from the man's shirt pocket and read from it. "Receipt for a pair of boots from a store in Oklahoma. That and a few dollars is all that's on him."

"It doesn't matter. Nobody talked and nobody overheard. Whoever had Daddy killed might well know I'd try to find Amos Dillon. Somebody expected me to go looking for Amos and was ready."

"Maybe and maybe not," Fargo said.

"Maybe not?" Ellen frowned.

"A passing hawk sees a baby chick and it swoops down," Fargo said.

"You saying maybe he wasn't out to stop me from finding Amos?" Ellen frowned.

"That's right. Maybe he was just passing through. You'll not be knowing which it was. Get your horse and I'll see you home," Fargo said.

Ellen rose beside him wrapped in her own thoughts and there was still daylight hanging in the air when they reached the road that skirted the base of the hills. They followed the road and were about to turn off when he saw the buckboard coming toward them and recognized the driver. He halted and waited as Alicia rolled to a stop, her glance filled with questions as she took in Ellen and Fargo.

"My, what an unexpected surprise," she said, a slight edge in her voice. "I spent the afternoon visiting with Clara at the Dixon place."

"I was up in the Smokey Hills," Ellen said, and told what had happened in short, flat sentences.

Alicia peered at her when she finished. "How stupid of you to go up into the hills alone," she commented.

"I've often done it. This time things happened. Maybe on purpose," Ellen said darkly. "Maybe somebody didn't want me looking to find Amos." Alicia's eyes went to Fargo and he shrugged. "Fargo thinks the man was maybe just passing through," Ellen conceded.

"I imagine that's the truth of it," Alicia said, and returned her eyes to Fargo. "It'll be dark in ten minutes. You can't find cattle trails in the dark."

"True enough. I'll start again, come morning," he said.

"Stop by. I ate late with Clara, but I'm sure George

47

can whistle up something warm for you," Alicia said.

"Much obliged." Fargo nodded and Alicia flicked the reins and the buckboard rolled on.

"I can make it home from here," Ellen said stiffly. She fell silent at his glance and stayed that way as he rode beside her to her place. "Thank you, for everything," she said, the defensiveness gone from her voice.

He kept his face stern. "You still want help?" he asked severely, and she nodded. "Then you wait till I get back. No more searching in the hills."

"All right," she said, but his lake-blue eyes continued to probe. "Promise," she murmured, and he nodded acceptance and watched her take the light bay into the barn before he rode off. She was headstrong but she'd been shaken. It would hold her till he got back. He hoped, he added with a snort.

He took a low hill that cut distance, and when he moved downward, he saw the Johnson ranch spread out in the moonlight, the big main house lighted and everything else dark.

Alicia opened the door at his knock, clad in a dark-green, floor-length housecoat that buttoned down the front. The top buttons had been left open and the fullness of her breasts rose up with soft-cream curves. "Come in. George has a hot roast-beef sandwich waiting for you," she said, and led him into a study where a small plate with a silver cover rested on an end table with a shot glass of whiskey beside it. Alicia lowered herself onto a small settee alongside him with a whiskey glass of her own. "I imagined you could use a drink after what happened in the hills," she said.

"That's as good a reason as any." Fargo smiled and took a long draw of the whiskey. It was smooth and rich to the palate. "Good whiskey and good company, the rewards of life," he said.

"There are others," Alicia said.

"So there are," Fargo agreed between bites.

"I'm sorry you had to risk your life today," Alicia said.

"Wasn't the first time. Won't be the last," Fargo answered.

"Nevertheless, Ellen was very lucky you were near. I hope you could talk some sense into her. She can be a very difficult young woman."

"She just wants to find the truth about what happened," Fargo said.

"I want that, too, but not at the expense of other people's lives. And Ellen is quick to toss accusations. You know that nothing makes for bad feeling in a community like loose talk and innuendo," Alicia said.

"That's so," Fargo agreed.

"You understand. You see where others only look and you read more than trails. You read people. That's a gift," Alicia said.

"There are all kinds of trails." Fargo smiled.

"I don't imagine you'd take a permanent job," Alicia said. "You do what you're hired to do and move on."

"That's pretty much it," Fargo said, and finished the sandwich and the whiskey.

Alicia let herself look rueful. "Too bad. I could use someone like you here. The ranch foreman Tom had is way past his best days. Tom just couldn't let him go," she said.

"Sounds like your husband was a man of sentiment," Fargo said.

"Sometimes too much so," Alicia said. "There's no sense in climbing into the hills to bed down. Stay the night and enjoy a good sleep in a real bed and leave, come morning."

"All right. I'll take that invitation," Fargo said, and Alicia rose and showed him to a guest room with thick carpeting and a big four-poster bed. She waited while he unsaddled the Ovaro and brought his things in. "I appreciate this," he said.

"Anytime you want, Fargo. You're going to look for a trail through the Smokey Hills for me," Alicia said.

"You're paying me for that," he returned.

"Yes, but you could've turned me down and gone on. You got those three killers. You could've made that enough," she said.

"Never turn down a good job for good money," Fargo said.

Alicia smiled. "Or a good meal or a warm woman, if I'm quoting correctly."

"You are," he said.

"Sleep well," Alicia said, laughing, a low, pleasant sound.

He watched the way her full rear filled the housecoat as she left. Alone in the room, he undressed and slid under the sheet, enjoying the smooth touch of it against his body. He still had the lamp on low when he heard the faint knock on the door.

"Come in," he called, and sat up, the sheet falling down to just cover his groin as Alicia entered. She wore a cream-colored silk nightgown, the lacy neckline just managing to cover the deep fullness of her breasts. She came to the bed and sat down on the edge of the mattress. He saw her eyes take in the muscled smoothness of his torso. Her smile came slowly, a privacy inside it.

"I didn't come as a warm woman," she said softly.

"But you are one, I'm thinking," Fargo said as the edge of the lace neckline let him see the brown-pink curve of one small circle.

"That may be so, but that's not why I'm here. I came to tell you that I'm not like Ellen," Alicia Johnson said.

"That doesn't need telling," Fargo said dryly, and her smile widened.

"What I mean is that you decide there's nothing more to be found out about the killings and move on, I'll understand. I won't be asking you to waste your time chasing shadows," she said.

"Fair enough." Fargo nodded.

"I still think you'll find it was just a random, vicious robbery, but in any case . . ." She let words trail off as she leaned over and he felt her lips on his and smelled the faint perfume and powder of her. Her breasts were warm against his chest. "That's for caring enough to try," she murmured, and pulled away. She stood up, straightened, and her breasts pulled the top of the nightgown tight. "There is so much you can't be expected to understand. Perhaps when you come back we can talk more," she said.

"Why not?" he said as she left and closed the door behind her. He lay back, turned off the lamp, and the darkness enveloped him. The vicious killing of Doc Schubert had been more than it seemed. He was convinced of that, whether he'd be able to prove it or not. But other things were certainly not what they seemed, either. Clay Springs was a place of secrets, he decided as he closed his eyes and embraced sleep.

The soft bed made for a comfortable night and he was in the saddle an hour later than he'd planned with the dawn sun already over the hills. He rode north toward the Smokey Hills when he spied the lone horse and rider standing atop a hillock. The new sun caught the sheen of the light bay's coat. He changed direction and climbed to the top of the hillock. "You're up real early," he said as he drew to a halt.

"Satisfying curiosity," Ellen said stiffly.

"I was invited. A good night's sleep in a real bed appealed to me," he said.

"That's all?" she sniffed, with one thin eyebrow lifting.

"Yes," he snapped.

"Just be patient," she slid back icily.

His eyes narrowed at the young woman. "I'd figured you were resentful. That didn't take much to see. Then I thought maybe you and your stepmother just didn't get along. Now I'm wondering if you're plain jealous," Fargo said.

"Go to hell," Ellen exploded. "I may be a lot of things but that's not one of them."

"Then stop sounding like it," Fargo threw back, and saw the anger go from her face.

"I'm sorry. I guess I just can't help it," she said.

"I won't buy that. That's too easy," Fargo said, and she blinked at him.

"You don't give any, do you?" she muttered.

"Not for excuses."

"There's a lot you don't understand. Maybe if you stay around long enough you will."

"I'll help try to find out about the killings. That's all I'm interested in. Now get the hell home," Fargo said darkly, and she turned the bay and rode away. He waited until she was out of sight before he rode on. He'd been purposely harsh. He didn't intend to be drawn into personal conflicts that didn't bear on the killing of Doc

Schubert. Besides, experience had taught him that those things were best left untouched.

He spurred the Ovaro forward and the sun was full and high when he climbed west along the Smokey Hills. He rode horizontally through the lower hills, climbed higher, and finally halted, his lips pulled back in a grimace. Once again, the hills remained dense with tree cover. Where they opened, the land rose and dipped too much to drive cattle.

He found a place under a pair of thick red oak to bed down and slept as soon as he'd eaten the beef jerky from his saddlebags. He rode eastward along the high hills and explored the east end of the hills, crossing and recrossing the terrain. He slowly made his way downward into the low hills as night came. The next day he again rode the lower hills back and forth, and when night came, he was moving out of the Smokey Hills onto the softly rolling land below. He had gone over damn near every foot of the land without finding a trail fit for more than a half-dozen horses at a time. It had been slow and painstaking riding, constantly moving up and down the narrow hill passages from low to high hills and back again, taking care not to miss a section that suddenly came open.

But there hadn't been any and he rode through the early night toward Alicia Johnson's place. He was glad to see the lights still on when he reached it.

Alicia opened the door in a dark-blue silk robe, surprise in her eyes when she saw him that instantly turned to welcome. "You look tired," she observed as he stepped into the house.

"A little. Three days on hill riding gets to you," Fargo admitted. Alicia hurried to a cabinet and took out glasses and whiskey. He enjoyed the feel of the

53

warm, bracing liquid as it seeped through his body. "I'm sorry I haven't anything good to tell you," Fargo said. "There's no place to drive a herd through those hills."

Alicia took his words with a philosophic shrug and a sip from her glass of whiskey. "Well, I had to be sure," she said.

"Fact is, I'm a little surprised that your husband didn't know that, having gone into the Smokey Hills and lived his life here," Fargo said.

Alicia smiled. "The only part of the Smokies he ever went into was the lower east area when he went visiting Amos. He disliked those hills with a vengeance. Tom was never a man for uncomfortable riding," she said. "Which brings me to you. I'll bet you'd enjoy a hot bath and a good bed after three days in those hills."

"It sure sounds good," Fargo admitted.

"Then it's done. We've a good bath and I'll have George fill it with hot water while you bring your things in," Alicia said. "I appreciate you having taken three days to do so thorough a job." She rose quickly and the top of the robe opened enough for Fargo to glimpse the full swell of one creamy breast as she hurried from the room. He rose and brought his things in after unsaddling the pinto to find the bathtub ready for him in a large bathroom half done in tile. Alicia appeared as he was about to start shedding clothes. "Take your time. I'll be waiting downstairs when you've finished," she said.

He nodded, closed the door, took off clothes, and sank into the porcelain tub. The hot water flowed around his body with a warm, delicious embrace and he luxuriated in its soothing comfort. He lingered, soaped and rinsed, and finally, about to rise, he looked around for the towels and saw only the empty towel rack. He was still frowning when he heard the rap on the door. "Come in," he said, and the door opened to Alicia, two big towels folded across her arms.

"I'm sorry, I forgot to put the towels in," she said, her brown eyes moving quickly across the upper part of his body out of the bathwater. "Force of habit," she said, and Fargo questioned with a frown. "Tom suffered from bad arthritis sometimes. He liked me to come in and dry him off. Of course, you're not in need of that," she added as she halted by the towel rack.

"I'm not in need of it, but it sounds great," Fargo said. Alicia paused, put down one towel, and let the other unfold as she walked toward him. He rose from the bathwater and she draped the big towel around him as he stepped from the tub. She began to dry him, his face and neck, first, then his shoulders, his chest then, her hands strong, rubbing with firm, vigorous motions. Her hands dropped lower, across his muscled abdomen, down along the powerful bulges of his thighs, and all the while her eyes never left his. But as her hands moved across his groin, his organ already responding, she touched him. He saw her lips part, her breath came in a quick, sharp intake of air. The towel dropped and his arms rose, hands pulling the robe open to curl around the full softness of her breasts.

"Oh, Jesus," Alicia breathed as his fingers rubbed across large, deep-pink nipples on surprisingly modest circles. "Oh, Jesus," she echoed as he pushed the robe from her, and his thrustingness pushed into her, soft-hard against the wiry nap of her. "Not here," Alicia breathed, and turned, one arm wrapped around him as she led him from the bathroom, across the corridor, to a large bedroom, dimly lighted and hung with deep-blue drapes. She moved to a large double-sized bed and fell onto it to stare up at him, her eyes moving up and down his body. He let her enjoy him as he took in a full figure, round hips, a little belly over a bushy black nap, and creamy skin, still-youthful thighs, and full, deep breasts that held their pillowiness without sagging.

Alicia Johnson was a woman of earthy sensuousness, a throbbing hunger exuding from her full-fleshed form. He sank down, pushing his face into the deep breasts, his mouth finding a large nipple. "Oh, yes . . . oh, Jesus, yes, yeeeeessss," Alicia cried out, one hand locking behind his neck to pull him deeper over her breast. He drew in the creamy softness, felt the nipple pulsate against the roof of his mouth, and heard Alicia scream with something close to wild laughter. His hand moved down across her body and she murmured throaty urgings, lifting her hips as he pressed down over the thick black nap. He slid his fingers through its denseness and felt the rise of her pubic mound.

The fleshy thighs parted, came together, and parted again, the flesh beckoning, and his hand moved to her and felt the dampness of her inner thighs that instantly snapped together around him. She held his hand in the creamy vise for a moment and then her thighs fell away. Alicia pushed her ample hips upward. He let his fingers caress. "Oh, Jesus, yes, oh, yes, damn, yes, yes . . . aaaaaiiiiii," Alicia cried, and groaned and half-cried again as he pushed deeper. He felt her hands clasp around his buttocks, digging into the flesh as she half-pulled, half-pushed him atop her. He let his maleness press flat against her and she rose, pushing her hips to one side, then the other, coming back again, seeking, wanting. Her throbbing hunger came with some surprise to him.

"Jesus, take me, take me, take me," Alicia called out, each phrase more urgent then the one before. He let himself slide forward to the wide and moist portal. Alicia screamed, this time a wild shuddering sound as he reached deep inside her. Her hands locked behind his neck again as she pulled his face against her breasts. She hissed ecstasy as his mouth enclosed one and then the other. Her belly was slapping against him, a soft, spongy sound as she thrust upward in short, spasmodic movements, and he half-turned and twisted inside her and she cried out with great, shuddering screams.

Suddenly the slapping against his groin grew faster and he felt himself being half-lifted as Alicia thrust her hips upward. He thrust hard into her and she was screaming as he felt her climax shatter, the peak of peaks explode and vanish all in one sublime moment. Alicia was still crying out "more" when she fell back on the bed, her full thighs still around him.

He lay with her and enjoyed the enveloping warm softness of her against him. Alicia Johnson was a lushly sensuous woman, he decided, a fact that transmitted itself even through the touch of her skin as it radiated its own special warmth. When he finally slid from her, he lay propped up on one elbow as she turned, her breasts pressing against him, their tips remaining large. Her eyes met his as a half-smile touched her lips. "You're wondering what kind of woman I am, having you only a week after my husband was murdered," she said.

"It passed my mind," he said.

"It's not callousness, it's starvation," Alicia said. "Tom wasn't able to make love for the last three years." Fargo's brows lifted as he listened. "I held back as best I could. It was hard, believe me. I'm a woman who needs being made love to. And then suddenly Tom is gone and someone like you comes along. I guess I just exploded, inside and outside.''

''I'd say so,'' Fargo agreed.

Alicia's hand came up to gently stroke his chest. ''You still going to stay to find out about the killings?'' she asked.

''I told Ellen I'd try to help find out.'' He nodded.

''Then help me, too,'' Alicia said. ''In another way. Come visit, whenever you can, whenever you want.'' Her hand tightened against his chest, moved down to cup him in her fingers.

''Why not?'' Fargo said. ''That'll be the good side of this.''

''Yes, yes, it will. I promise,'' Alicia said. She drew her hand up to encircle his chest as she cradled herself against him. He felt her body relax and she was fast asleep in minutes. He reached out and turned the lamp off and lay back. Unexpected pleasures, he smiled. They were always the best.

4

He woke with the morning, and when he'd finished in the bathroom, he found Alicia awake and sitting up in bed.

She held her arms out and he came to her and the softness of her breasts pressed into him. "Don't forget about coming back," she murmured.

"That'd be hard to do," he said.

"Meanwhile, I'll stick with Royd Haggard as the most likely to have engineered the killings, if you're right about them," Alicia said.

"I'm right," he grunted. "Ellen gave me a few others. Billy Harrison and Zach Traynor."

Alicia let her lips purse. "I didn't consider those." She frowned. She swung from the bed, pulled on a robe, and he finished dressing. "I'll keep thinking. Maybe I'll come up with somebody else. We can exchange notes when you visit."

"Good enough," he said, and left after a lingering kiss from Alicia's full lips. Some of the ranch hands were setting out feed for the cattle in the corrals as he rode from the ranch. He cut distance by climbing the low hills, and when he reached Ellen's place, he was surprised to see her outside, unsaddling the light bay. "You've been out riding already?" he asked.

"Every morning at dawn," she said, and his eyes narrowed.

"You promised you were going to stay out of the Smokey Hills," he said.

"I didn't say I wouldn't ride along the base of them," she returned with a trace of smugness. He stared sternly.

"I stayed along the base of the east section. That's where Amos lives. There were riders that went into the hills each morning looking for him, four of them."

"Recognize any?"

"No."

"How do you know they were looking for Amos Dillon?"

"I waited each day until they returned. No game, no pelts, no anything, and they weren't the type to go for an afternoon pleasure ride in the hills. Besides, I know it inside. They were looking for Amos," Ellen said with complete certainty.

Fargo turned her words in his mind. She could well be right, he realized. He wasn't one to dismiss inner feelings. "You see them this morning?" he asked.

"No," she said, apprehension clouding her face. "I'm afraid of what that means."

"You're thinking it means they found him yesterday," Fargo said, and she nodded unhappily. "Not necessarily. They could've given up. No one's going to keep looking forever."

"I suppose so." Ellen frowned. "God, I wanted to go up and look for him myself, but I kept my promise."

"Very commendable and very smart. It seems more people than you and Alicia knew about your pa's visits to Amos Dillon," Fargo said.

"That's probably so. Pa used to talk about visiting

Amos, and every two years or so Amos would make a trip into town,'' Ellen said.

"Saddle up again. Let's go look for ourselves,'' Fargo said.

"All right,'' Ellen agreed, excitement instant in her voice. He watched as she tightened the cinch and pulled herself onto the horse. Her willowy figure moved with supple ease, longish breasts swaying gracefully under a tan shirt. "He always met Daddy in one area the times I was along. I think they always met there,'' she said as he rode beside her at a fast trot. She led halfway up into the hills, and his gaze swept the terrain as he rode. He noted a long narrow bed of brilliant scarlet butterfly weed, the way in which two black oak trunks twined around each other, and a dense cluster of pokeweed. The place marked in his mind, he followed Ellen into the hollow between the two slopes. She halted and began to call out Amos' name. Fargo hung back as she circled the hollow, calling out for Amos Dillon, but there was no answer. Fargo saw the disappointment fill her face. She turned to face him as he came toward her.

"This is the place, I know it,'' Ellen said. "But let's go on into the next hollow.''

"You go on. I'm going to leave you,'' Fargo said, and then, quickly, as he saw the surprise in her eyes, "Only it'll just look like that. Maybe he'll come out if you're alone.''

Ellen nodded and he turned in a tight circle and slowly rode up the slope. When he reached the top, he looked back to see Ellen disappear down the far side of the next slope. He moved from the top of the slope, went a quarter of the way down, and dismounted. He placed the Ovaro in a thick clump of oak and hurried on foot back up the hillside until he could see Ellen as she circled the second hollow. Fargo crept forward, his eyes trained on both slopes as they swept the tree-covered slopes, moving slowly, carefully. He scanned the trees back and forth. He was about to turn away when he suddenly caught sight of movement in the foliage along a line of oaks. He watched and saw the leaves move again, the branches being brushed as someone moved on foot through the trees.

Fargo's eyes followed the path of the movement downhill as he crept forward on silent footsteps. He was starting down the second slope and he could see Ellen at the bottom of the hollow, not very far away. His eyes went back to the foliage. He was watching the branches move as a figure stepped out into the open—a tall, thin man in a tattered black jacket and black trousers. The man glanced up and down the slope, an old, long-barreled Kentucky plains rifle in one hand. Fargo saw a gray beard on a long face with eyes set in deep pockets that gave him a perpetually gaunt expression. His gray-brown hair hung to his shoulders but had been recently brushed.

Ellen swung her horse around as she saw him and came up the slope at once. "Amos," she called out as she halted and swung to the ground. The man held the rifle in the crook of his arm as he surveyed the young woman with an uncertain frown. "It's me, Amos," Ellen said.

"I know that," Amos Dillon said.

Fargo stepped from behind the trees, the Colt in hand. "Nobody's going to hurt you. Put the rifle down," he said softly, and Amos Dillon turned with the quickness of a man half his age. He saw the Colt aimed directly at him and lowered the barrel of the rifle.

"It's all right, Amos, he's a friend. He was trying to help me find you," Ellen said quickly. The old recluse peered at Fargo out of pale-blue eyes that carried a volume of personal shadows. Yet Fargo saw no resentment in them; only a sad acceptance. Fargo lowered the Colt and Amos Dillon turned back to Ellen.

"What are you doing up here, girl? Where's your pa?" he asked.

"Pa won't be coming to visit anymore, Amos," Ellen said gently, and told him what had happened.

Fargo watched Amos Dillon's face seem to crumple.

"Oh God, dear God," the old recluse murmured as he lowered himself onto a length of log. "Tom, Tom, my old friend, Tom. Damn the black souls in this world, damn them all."

"Fargo, here, thinks there's more to this than meets the eye," Ellen said.

The old recluse looked up, his light-blue eyes narrowing. "I wouldn't know about that, but there's been strangers searchin' all over these parts for me," he said.

"How do you know they were searching for you?" Fargo questioned.

"They were trying to pick up trails, lookin' into every thicket and cluster of trees. I'm the only one livin' up here. They had to be lookin' for me," the man said.

"Did Daddy tell you about the operation, Amos?" Ellen asked, and the man nodded. "Did he tell you anything else? He talk about having trouble with anyone?"

Fargo's eyes bored into the old recluse as the man brushed aside the question. "No, nothin' like that," Amos Dillon said.

"What did you talk about, Amos?" Ellen pressed.

"Just talk," Amos said, and Fargo's eyes stayed on him. The old man was being more than reticent.

"Just talk? All the times Daddy came to visit you, what did you talk about?" Ellen questioned.

"Old-times talk, that's all," Amos said. A turn-away answer, Fargo decided, but made no comment.

"Think, Amos, maybe he did tell you something last time. Think hard," Ellen persisted.

"I told you, we talked about the old days. That's what we always talked about," Amos bristled. He was holding back. Fargo was certain. Amos rose to his feet. "No more questions. I want to be alone with my own thinking about Tom," he said. Fargo's eyes stayed on Amos. The old recluse was upset. There was no doubt on that. But he was also nervous. He plainly didn't want any more questions from Ellen. Amos stayed in place and glanced from Fargo to Ellen and back again. "You can go your way," he said.

Fargo nodded at Ellen's glance, turned away, and climbed up the slope to where he'd left the Ovaro in the trees.

He waited for her as she rode up the hillside and swung in beside her. "Poor Amos. He was so upset. He didn't even want to talk to me," Ellen said. "I've never seen him like that. He was always so friendly to me when I was with Daddy."

"As you said, he was real upset," Fargo remarked, unwilling to share suspicions with Ellen until he'd thought more on his own.

The day was fading and disappointment clouded her face as they reached her place. "I so hoped Amos could help. What now?" she asked.

"I'll think some on it," Fargo said.

Ellen speared him with a sidelong glance. "I'll hire

you," she said. "I'll pay you to stay on and help me get to the bottom of this thing." He let his lips purse as he considered her offer. "You're finished with your job for Alicia, aren't you?" Ellen asked, and he nodded. "Then there's no reason you can't stay for me," Ellen said.

"None," he agreed, wisely silent about the reasons Alicia had given him for staying. "But no pay. I'll stay for Doc Schubert. He deserves the truth."

She peered at him. "If that's how you want it," she said. "But you get back to me, not Alicia."

His smile was edged with ice. "I don't take orders, honey," he said. "I'll get back to whoever I like, whenever I like. I won't leave Alicia out. Hell, she's got a right to know just as much as you do."

"No, not as much." Ellen frowned.

"But enough," Fargo said, and she accepted the answer in silence.

"What are you going to do now?"

"Make some smoke."

"And I just sit around waiting?"

"For now.'

"I don't like waiting."

"It's good for you. Builds character," he said as he rode away and darkness descended. He slowed when he was away from Ellen's place and rode slowly across the rolling land as his thoughts crystallized. Amos Dillon had been nervous, too nervous. Because of what Ellen had told him or because of what he knew? The question clung. There was another. Had he been nervous because of Ellen's presence? There seemed no reason for that, yet the thought persisted. He'd pay another visit to Amos Dillon, Fargo decided, alone. He'd ferret out the man, no matter how well he hid himself away, Fargo grunted. Meanwhile, he'd see what raising a little smoke might bring. He turned the horse toward Clay Springs.

When he reached the town, the CLAY SPRINGS PLAYHOUSE was an oasis of sound and light in the otherwise darkened town. He tethered the Ovaro to the end of the hitching post outside and stepped into the saloon, where he scanned a typically large room, a bar along one side and tables against the other three walls. A half-dozen bar girls sauntered through the room, all in low-cut dresses that showed too much for some of them. He saw a woman atop a high stool at the far end of the bar. Her tightly curled hair had a brassy shine to it and powder and paint were unable to mask the weariness in her face. She was in charge of the girls, he guessed.

The bar was fairly crowded, most of the men wearing ranch-hand work clothes. The bartender, a medium height, square-faced man in a white shirt and white apron, came over as Fargo found himself a spot at the bar. "Bourbon," Fargo ordered. "The drinkable kind." The bartender allowed a smile as he reached under the bar and brought out a bottle with a South Carolina label. The whiskey was pleasant, Fargo found as he took the first sip. "Just passing through, stranger?" the bartender asked.

"Not anymore," Fargo said in a firm, clear voice. "I came for a visit and now I'm looking for a damn murderer." He took another draw of the bourbon and knew his answer had every pair of ears at the bar listening.

"You talking about what happened at Doc Schubert's?" The bartender frowned.

"That's right," Fargo said, and noted that the

murmur of voices at the bar had dropped almost to silence.

"I heard that the three who did it had been killed," the bartender said.

"I know. I was there," Fargo said, the answer saying more than the mere words, and he smiled inwardly. The bar had fallen entirely silent, along with a few of the nearest tables.

"But you just said you were looking for a murderer." The bartender frowned.

"Those three were hired guns. It was no robbery. The way I see it, somebody ordered that killing."

The bartender's face stayed sober. "Strong words, mister," he said.

"Guess so, but somebody wanted Tom Johnson dead. You know anybody that might've had reasons?" Fargo asked.

"No, no, I wouldn't know that," the man said quickly, and Fargo smiled inwardly. He hadn't expected an answer.

"I've some names I'm going to check out. You think of anyone, you let me know next time I stop by," Fargo said as he finished the drink.

"I'll do that," the man said, and Fargo strolled from the bar. The talk would erupt when he left, he knew, and talk traveled. By tomorrow there'd be damn few people in the nearby territory that wouldn't know of his conversation with the bartender. He'd sent up the smoke. It was the first step. Sometimes the only way to flush out a hiding fox was little by little. Fargo found a spot to bed down under the veined leaves of a big black oak, slept soundly, and allowed himself an extra hour of leisure when morning came. He washed at a small stream and then slowly made his way down to a winding dirt road.

He ambled along the road until he came onto a man driving a yellow-wheeled fruit-rack wagon filled with gourds and squashes. The driver reined to a halt and by the time Fargo ended his casual questioning he had all the information he wanted for the moment. His first goal took him southward, along the edge of a long, low hill, and finally to the widespread layout that was the Royd Haggard ranch. He approached at a slow walk and took in a low-roofed main house of imposing proportions. A half-dozen ranch hands watched him as he drew up in front of the house and three more men stepped from around a corner of the house and came toward him. One, a tall man with a frowning face and short black hair, came to a halt as the door of the house opened and a figure stepped outside.

Fargo stayed in the saddle as the figure stepped closer, a big man with brown hair just beginning to gray, a face that radiated authority and power. A large, jutting jaw and hard blue eyes, lips firmly set. It was a face that made no effort to concede to amiability or softness. "Royd Haggard?" Fargo asked, the question mere formality.

Royd Haggard's hard eyes speared into the big man astride the Ovaro. "You're the one," he slid out of lips that barely moved.

"Am I?" Fargo returned.

"Yes. One of my men said you rode a fine-looking Ovaro," Royd Haggard said. "You've nerve coming here, I'll give you that."

"Why's that?"

"After your talk at the bar? Hell, everybody knows

I hated Tom Johnson. That makes me one of those suspects of yours,'' Royd Haggard said, his voice rising.

"I guess it does."

"Goddamn," Royd Haggard breathed, a kind of angry awe in his voice.

The tall man with short black hair stepped forward. "Let me blow his damn head off, Royd," he said.

"No, that'd sure start folks wondering even more," Haggard said. There was intelligence underneath the man's overbearing mien, Fargo realized.

"It would that," Fargo agreed. "And leave you without a foreman."

"You son of a bitch," the man exploded as his hand flew to his holster. He had the gun clear of the holster when the big Colt barked in Fargo's hand. The man cursed in pain as he grabbed his right forearm and the gun dropped from his hand.

"That could've been between your eyes," Fargo said. "But I try to be kind to drunks and damn fools."

The man, still cursing, bent over as he held his arm.

"Take him to Doc Dawson in Hillsdale," Royd Haggard said with more annoyance than sympathy, and two men stepped forward to help the foreman away. Royd Haggard's cold eyes returned to Fargo. "Why'd you come here?" he asked.

"Wanted to hear about you and Tom Johnson," Fargo said.

"That's bullshit," Royd Haggard snapped. "You came to throw out bait and have a look at me for yourself." Fargo smiled. Haggard was not without his own acuity. "You see what you came to see?" the man asked.

"I'm satisfied," Fargo said.

"Meaning what?" Haggard pressed.

"You could've done it," Fargo answered, his eyes meeting Royd Haggard's stare.

"I could've, but I didn't," the man said.

"Don't expect you'd say anything different," Fargo returned.

"Get off my land, Fargo," the man said, his powerful jaw thrust out. "You're playing games with the wrong man."

"Likewise," Fargo said as he turned the pinto and walked the horse with slow deliberation. There had been an icy exchange and that would hold for now. Royd Haggard had all the arrogance of power and he was smart. But what he wouldn't realize was that his reaction, no matter what it was, would send its own message. Fargo put the Ovaro into a trot and headed north. He skirted Clay Springs and, following the directions the man in the fruit wagon had given him, came to a ranch with plenty of corral space but none of the impressiveness of the Haggard place. Or the Johnson spread, he added. A man fixing the wheel of a buckboard stopped his work and came forward.

"You Ben Hart?" Fargo asked and the man nodded.

"I was told Zach Traynor is working for you," Fargo said.

"Most of the year," the man said. "What do you want with him?"

"Alicia Johnson wants me to ask him a few questions," Fargo said, the answer only half a lie.

"That's him at the end of the west corral fence," the man said.

"Much obliged." Fargo nodded and sent the Ovaro along the weathered fence of the corral at his right.

Zach Traynor looked up from mending a fencepost.

As Fargo approached, the man's small eyes narrowed. Zach Traynor had a wispy mustache and a mouth that turned down at the corners to give him a sour expression. "Name's Fargo . . . Skye Fargo," the Trailsman said. "Came to have a few words."

"About the killing at Doc Schubert's place?" Zach Traynor asked, and Fargo nodded. "I expected a visit when I heard somebody was snooping around about it."

"Tom Johnson fired you. You talked about getting even with him for it," Fargo said.

"Talking's not the same as doing," Zach Traynor growled.

"One can turn into the other," Fargo said.

"You got something that says it did?" the man asked belligerently.

"Not yet."

"Then stay the hell away from me, 'less you want to end same as Tom Johnson."

"That could sound like you're admitting something."

"That's a warning for you, that's all," the man barked. He was a hollow man full of braggadocio, Fargo sensed, but even hollow men could be dangerous. His eyes moved across Zach Traynor, saw a gun belt of cracked leather, a holster of frayed hide, boots badly in need of replacing, and patched Levi's. He made his own mental notes as he backed the pinto a half-dozen paces.

"If you weren't involved, you've no worries. If I find you were, you're a dead man," Fargo said quietly, and turned the pinto around. He rode calmly from the ranch as he felt the man's eyes bore into him. He had one more visit to make, and once again following the directions he had been given, he found his way to Ridge Hill. The place was well-named—a hill traversed with tree lined ridges rising sharply behind a small shack. He halted alongside a line of black oak as he surveyed the shack, a run-down place with the front door hanging by a single hinge and a hole in one corner of the roof.

The shack was silent, nothing moving in or around it that he could discern. His eyes narrowed as he scanned the ridged and tree-covered hill, and he felt the back of his neck suddenly tingle. At a firm pressure of his knee and the inner part of his thigh, the Ovaro instantly moved sideways, a maneuver few horses could execute. As he slipped into the trees, the shot rang out, rifle fire, and he heard the bullet whistle through the leaves. He drew farther into the trees as a second shot slammed into a nearby branch. He was out of the shooter's sight, but he could see the shack through the leaves. It remained a still and silent place. The shots had come from one of the ridges along the hill. Suddenly he heard the sound of a horse galloping away.

Being cautious, he waited another moment before he nosed out of the trees as the hoofbeats died away. The rifleman had gotten away, probably along one of the ridges. Fargo's lips pursed. Apparently Billy Harrison didn't welcome visitors. If it had been Billy Harrison, Fargo murmured to himself. He wouldn't be jumping to conclusions about anyone, though his guess was that it was Harrison. He slowly rode toward the shack, the Colt in his hand. He halted in front of the hanging door, dismounted, and stepped into the shack. Clothes and unwashed pots and pans showed it was a place being lived in. He picked a shirt from the floor and held it up. Billy Harrison was on the small side. He let the shirt drop and moved from the shack to stand for a moment outside, his eyes sweeping the rise of the ridged hill that all but surrounded the house.

Finally, he remounted and rode away as the day began to draw to an end. He stopped at the Johnson ranch on his way to town and Alicia greeted him outside with proper decorum and inside with a throbbing kiss and her breasts pushing hard into his chest. "Welcome back," she said.

"I can't stay tonight," he said, and she made a face. He told her of his commitment to Ellen and the visits he had made.

"I appreciate what you're doing. I just don't want to see you putting your life in danger. I've better plans than that in mind for you," Alicia said.

"That'll help me be careful," he answered.

Her arm linked into his as she walked to the door with him. "Promise me you'll give it up if you don't find any proof. Don't let Ellen keep you chasing shadows," Alicia said.

"I won't. I'm not much for that," he agreed.

"You killed the three who did it. Maybe we'll all have to make do with that," she said thoughtfully.

"Maybe," he conceded, and Alicia's lips found his, her kiss moist and inviting.

"Sure you won't stay?" she murmured.

"Can't. I started something. I've got to keep the fire going," he said, and pulled from her with an effort.

He rode toward Clay Springs as he struggled to convince himself of the virtues of being conscientious. The town was still and dark when he reached it, only the Clay Springs Playhouse an island of light. Inside, it hardly seemed changed from the night before, the woman with the tight curls seated atop the stool at the end of the bar, the girls mechanically circulating among the customers. But the bartender greeted him with open-faced curiosity as he poured a bourbon. "On the house," he said.

"Thanks." Fargo smiled but realized the drink was offered more as an encouragement to loosen his tongue than of amiability.

"You shook me up last night. Other folks, too," the bartender said. "We all figured what happened at Doc Schubert's was just a plain robbery. Then you come along and say it wasn't."

"Still say it," Fargo nodded.

"Got any more ideas on it?" the bartender asked. His eagerness to draw him out was hardly subtle, Fargo noted silently.

"Some. Went visiting. Asked questions," Fargo said.

"Such as?"

Fargo took a slow draw of his drink as the bar became almost silent. The bartender's ears were not the only ones tuned to his answer. "I'm not accusing anybody, but it's plain that Royd Haggard had the most to gain from Tom Johnson's death. It made him top rancher in these parts," Fargo said.

"I hear Alicia Johnson figures to go on running the place," the bartender said.

"It won't be the same, even if she does. She won't give Royd Haggard any real competition," Fargo said, and continued to expand his remarks. No direct accusations again, but he mentioned Zach Traynor and Billy Harrison in passing while he made Royd Haggard his definite number-one candidate. Some of the others at the bar asked direct questions, others remained silent listeners, and he noted a smallish figure at a nearby table paying silent but strict attention while nursing a beer.

The woman at the end of the bar on the high stool also clearly took in every word without changing the expressionless mask she wore. He ordered another bourbon and let the whiskey seem to make him more loquacious. Finally he paid for the drink and reiterated his determination to get at all the truth behind the killings.

"I'll stop by tomorrow night. Maybe I'll have something more to tell you," he said to the bartender, making certain his voice was loud and clear before strolling from the saloon with just the touch of a swagger.

Once outside, the swagger dropped from his shoulders and his eyes were narrowed as he climbed onto the Ovaro. Royd Haggard would hear about his remarks in the bar, he was certain. He'd be prepared for the man's reaction, whatever it was. Fargo rode into the low hills again and bedded down, slept quickly, and woke when morning brightened the land. He spent the morning on another, more careful visit to Billy Harrison's shack, halting in the trees to survey the shack and scan the ridged hill behind. Nothing moved at either place. He rode forward, slipped from the horse, and crossed the cleared ground on foot to step into the shack, his eyes sweeping the small room. Billy Harrison had been there during the night. The leftovers of fresh food on a tin plate and the disarranged clothes piled on the floor proved that.

Billy Harrison had returned in the night and hurried away before the dawn came. He was unwilling or not ready to face him. Why? Fargo wondered. Fear of the past rising up in his face? Or fear of something more recent? Or just natural caution? He was still wanted by the authorities in the New Mexico Territory. Maybe he simply hoped to stay out of sight until everything blew over. Then maybe he had a lot more reason to stay hidden.

Fargo juggled the thoughts for a moment longer before putting them aside. But Billy Harrison was making himself into a major question mark. The youth was deserving of more attention, Fargo thought as he paused in the doorway before stepping outside. He listened, scanned the ridged hill again, and finally stepped into the clear. He halted beside a set of hoofprints, knelt, and pressed his hands into the indented marks.

They were fresh, the soil still damp to the touch, confirmation of what he had found inside the shack. He climbed onto the Ovaro and rode away, crossed a low hill, and went out of his way to pass the Ben Hart ranch, where Zach Traynor was still mending fenceposts. Fargo made sure the man saw him as he halted and, with slow deliberateness, let his gaze pause on Zach Traynor. He peered at the man for a full minute as Traynor glared back from the other side of the corral. Finally, Fargo moved the pinto on and rode slowly from the ranch, not looking back but aware that Zach Traynor still glared after his receding figure. The silent visit would make Traynor even more nervous than he was already, Fargo knew. It was a dangerous cat-and-mouse game he had started, Fargo realized, with himself as the central target. But it was the only way to trigger reactions that would help tell him the things he needed to know.

The afternoon had started to slide toward dusk when he turned toward Ellen's place. She was outside and had just finished filling a feed trough when he rode up. She came forward to meet him, clad in Levi's and a denim work shirt—still a picture of slender loveliness.

But her thin black eyebrows were lowered and her face was set stiffly. "You stopped to see Alicia last night. She came by this morning," Ellen said, accusation in her voice.

"So I did. Something wrong in that?" Fargo said.

"You don't have to report to her," Ellen said, and somehow managed to sound hurt as well as icy.

"Damn, you've thorns on that tongue of yours," Fargo said. "I didn't report. I told you I wouldn't leave her out of it. She has a right to know."

"You spend the night again?" Ellen asked, resentment in the light-blue eyes.

"No, not that it's any of your business," Fargo said.

"I suppose not," she conceded without agreeing. "It just brings up bad memories."

He studied her for a moment. Anger and protectiveness were very much inside her, as much as if her father were still alive. He didn't want to violate a confidence, but perhaps it was time Ellen was given something to think about. "You're talking about Alicia and your pa, of course," he said, and her silence was an admission. "Maybe there are things you don't know."

"Maybe there are things I do know about and maybe some people are good at convenient lies," Ellen tossed back.

"One thing's for sure. Your pa wanted Alicia enough to marry her. Seems to me that ought to mean something to you," Fargo said. "I think you ought to accept that."

"She wound her way around him when he was lonely and vulnerable. He couldn't see through her," Ellen returned adamantly.

"But you could," Fargo commented.

"Damn right," she snapped. He held back further

answers. There was no give in her. The enmity had roots too deep for words to dispel, no matter how reasonable they were. Not now, anyway. Perhaps time and events would make her see things differently, Fargo reflected as he drew a deep breath.

"Meanwhile, you keep your door latched, come dark, just in case." he said.

"You stop by to tell me that?" she asked.

"I did," he said, and saw her face soften.

"Thanks," she said. "That was nice of you."

"Don't let it go to your head, honey. I'm on my way to tell Alicia the same thing," he said.

Ellen's lips tightened instantly. "Of course," she said, spun on her heels, and strode into the house.

He rode on and found himself speculating on the depths of Ellen's bitterness toward Alicia. He couldn't help wondering if Alicia had been less than discreet and perhaps not nearly as starved for affection as she had led him to believe. If Ellen knew, that would be more than enough to turn dislike into hatred. It was damn unlikely she'd ever believe Alicia's reason, even if she suspected there could be truth in it. Loyalty and love prevent that. Fargo dismissed the thoughts. Their personal problems didn't affect what he had to do. He reached the Johnson ranch as night fell.

Alicia answered at his knock and a wry smile touched her lips as she peered at him. "Same as last night. You're not staying," she said.

"Bull's-eye." He nodded.

"You just come by to tantalize me?" she asked.

"I stopped by to tell you to keep your door latched. Chances are it's assumed I'm working for you or Ellen on this," he said. "I can't be sure what I might trigger."

"All right," Alicia said. "You warn Ellen?"

"I did."

"Good. I can't hate her the way she hates me," Alicia said.

Fargo smiled. "That's nice of you, but then you don't have any reasons, do you?" he said.

The comment drew a slow smile from Alicia. "Is that a note of sympathy I detect? Has little Ellen been reaching you?"

"No, I just like to keep the record straight," Fargo said.

"I like that, too. All right, she's the aggrieved daughter and I'm the wicked stepmother. Is that straight enough?" Alicia said, her smile staying.

"I didn't mean that," Fargo said quickly. Alicia was quick and assured, unafraid to poke fun at herself and come off the better for it. She was quite a woman, he decided as her arms slid around his neck and her lips were moist and soft on his. "Maybe I can come back later," he said, her pillowy breasts warm against his chest. "Maybe."

"I'll be here," Alicia said.

5

A three-quarter moon lighted his way and he took the road into Clay Springs. He smiled as he thought about the difference between Alicia and Ellen. No glowering resentment for Alicia, not even at the dig he'd given her. A dozen or more years to mature made the difference, he reflected. One was still made of fiery, girlish immaturity, the other a woman in touch with herself. Contrasts. Perhaps one more reason Ellen resented Alicia so. He snapped off these thoughts as he reached Clay Springs.

The scene inside the saloon seemed much the same, with perhaps a few more men at the bar and nearby tables. The bartender had a bourbon poured for him before he reached the bar. The woman sat and watched from the far end.

"Anything new to tell?" the bartender asked, his square face filled with eager curiosity.

"Nothing real new," Fargo said. "Nothing that's changed my mind any, especially about Royd Haggard." He settled against the bar with his drink and let himself grow loquacious again, expanding on the reliability of motive and opportunity. He noticed two men walk past him. The second of the two suddenly stopped as Fargo took another pull on his bourbon.

"I don't like what you've been saying about my boss, mister," he heard the man growl and he turned to take in a man of medium height, slack-jawed with a puffy face. The man's small eyes bored into him.

"That'd be Royd Haggard, I take it," Fargo said as he straightened and faced the man.

"That's right," the man said, and before Fargo could say anything further a powerful blow smashed into the back of his neck. Fargo felt the searing pain shoot upward into his head as he staggered forward and dropped to one knee. He managed to half-turn and saw the other man with a club in his hand. He tried to duck away, but the world was swimming. He saw the club come down again as he managed to get one arm partly raised, but the club smashed past his forearm and onto the side of his head and he fell to the floor. The world was dissolving and pain shot through his body. He felt more than saw his gun yanked from its holster and he shook his head as a dog shakes water from its coat.

The world stopped dissolving for a moment, just long enough for him to see the boot that smashed into his ribs, to send him sprawling across the floor. The world was dissolving again when the ice-cold water struck him in the face, brutally reviving, and the saloon snapped back into focus. He was on his back and looking up at the brassy-haired woman with the water pitcher still in her hand. "Obliged," he bit out as he started to get up and saw the two men rushing at him, one still holding the club.

Fargo flung himself sideways and rolled to get under the nearest table. He almost made it when the club came crashing down across the back of his legs. Despite the rush of pain that swept through him, he kept rolling, drew his legs up, and got under the table. He swung himself around there and saw the club swept across the floor in an effort to reach him.

"Get back. I'll get us the bastard," he heard one of the men roar.

Fargo rose to one knee as he heard the smash of fists against wood and the round table upended. But Fargo was charging forward, driving with all his strength, one shoulder lowered and thrust forward. He slammed into the underside of the upended table, drove it forward, and saw the two men go down as the table smashed into them. He skirted around the table as it teetered on its broad edge, and saw the two men starting to regain their feet. His kick caught the nearest one alongside the head and the man's face spurted blood as he went down again. But the other one was charging with the club upraised. Fargo automatically put up one arm to parry the blow and then pulled it back as he realized the club could shatter his forearm. His back and legs were already sending waves of pain through him.

He held his position for a split second longer. His eyes watched the club as it began to sweep through the air to crash into his face. At the last second, he dropped down almost to his hands and knees and felt the swish of air as the club passed over the top of his head. He came up driving a short, left uppercut that landed alongside the man's jaw. The figure staggered sideways and Fargo followed with an upward lunge, both hands closing around the club. Ignoring the pain in his back, he twisted with both arms and the man staggered backward as the club was wrenched from his hands. Fargo started forward, the club raised to smash into his assailant, when a shot rang out and he felt the bullet tear through the side of his shirt and the instant trickle of blood down his side.

Another shot would follow if he tried to turn, he realized, and that one could do more than graze his ribs. He let the club fall from his hand as he collapsed to the floor, let himself fall onto his stomach, one side of his face hitting the wood of the floor. He lay there, his eyes closed, one arm stretched out motionlessly. "Goddamn, the boss said not to kill him," Fargo heard the nearest man call out. "Just beat him into a damn pulp."

"I don't care what the boss said. The son of a bitch split my cheekbone," the other one rasped.

Fargo stayed motionless and listened to the sound of the two men walk closer to stand over him. His eyes still seemed closed, but he could see through narrowed slits and saw the two pairs of legs and feet standing side by side. He tightened the muscles of his outstretched arm, snapped it sideways with all his strength, and his hands wrapped around the ankles of the man at his left. He pulled and heard the man's curse of surprise as he went over backward. Fargo flung his body in a half-roll and slammed into the second man's ankles hard enough to knock him off-balance and give him a few more precious seconds.

He twisted, winced at the pain in his back, and drove himself up onto his feet as he lunged forward. The man was bringing his gun up as Fargo slammed into him and the shot went wild. Fargo got one hand around the man's wrist, twisted hard as he drove forward, and the man cursed in pain as the pistol fell from his fingers. Fargo kept driving the man backward when he felt the knee come up into his groin and it was his turn to gasp in pain. He felt his grip loosen, his assailant twist away as he went down on one knee, grimaced there in pain for a moment. The man was diving for the six-gun, which had skittered a dozen feet across the floor. Fargo's hand flew to the calf-holster around his leg and pulled out the double-edged throwing knife. He turned as the man reached the gun with one outstretched hand, drew the pistol to him, and rose to one knee as he brought the gun up to fire. But the thin, razor-sharp blade was already hurtling through the air as Fargo threw it with a quick, underhand motion.

The man's eyes widened as he saw the flash of metal almost upon him. He tried to twist away but the blade impelled itself into the side of his neck, halting only when it reached the hilt. The man fell forward, a wheezing sound coming from his open mouth as he hit the floor and jerked spasmodically. But Fargo had already turned and pushed to his feet to face the other man, who charged at him with the club in his hand again. But this time the man's slack-jawed face darkened as he saw his partner on the floor, and he flung the club at Fargo with a roar of rage. Fargo ducked away from the flying length of wood and saw the man yanking at his gun. He threw himself forward in a low tackle, his arms wrapping around the man's legs. The tackle carried his opponent down and backward, but the man managed to get the gun up enough to fire a shot and Fargo felt the bullet graze his temple. A sharp, searing pain instantly spread through one side of his face, but he was atop the man on the floor now and got his left hand over the man's gun arm so that the next shot went up into the ceiling.

Fargo drove his right forearm into the man's throat with all the weight and strength left in him and felt the man's trachea crush into itself. The form under him went limp and a hoarse, rasping sound came from the man as Fargo pulled himself away. The man turned onto his side, his legs drawing up as he tried to find breath, the hoarse rasping sound from his throat now a terrible, harsh wheezing. It stopped in another few moments and the man lay still. Fargo straightened, fought off the attack of dizziness, and grimaced the pain that shot through his head and body. He turned, swept the now-silent onlookers with eyes still ice-cold despite the pain in them. He slowly stepped to the other man and retrieved his throwing knife. The woman at the end of the bar tossed him a lace kerchief and he wiped the blade clean before returning the blade to the calf holster.

He spotted the Colt on the floor against the bar and slowly walked to the gun, fought off another attack of dizziness as he bent over and picked up the weapon. He holstered the gun, straightened, and grimaced with the pain that shot through his body. But he had things to do. Royd Haggarad had tried to deliver a message. He'd return his own, Fargo swore silently as he stepped to the one silent form and began to drag it across the floor to where the second man lay. He paused when he reached the second man, drew in a deep breath, and shook away a wave of pain that surged through him.

He took hold of the shirt collar of the second man and began to slowly pull both figures toward the door of the saloon. The others in the bar looked on and began to move through the door as Fargo neared it with his silent baggage. Grimacing in pain, his neck a burning knot of muscles from the very first blow of the club, he dragged the two figures from the saloon. Once outside, he paused, straightened up to see that the others were all beside their horses, leaving only two mounts and the Ovaro. Fargo dragged the two figures to the horses, lifted first one and then the other to put each across the saddle facedown. He went to the Ovaro and groaned in pain as he pulled himself into the saddle. He paused to draw in another deep breath and then took the reins of the other two horses in hand and moved down the dark and silent street. He heard the others start to file back into the bar as he drew away, and he kept the pinto at a slow walk out of town. He stayed at the same pace as he moved down the road and took a low hill that cut time and distance from his journey.

He halted at least a half-dozen times to let some of the pain in his back subside for a few minutes before moving on again. The moon was far past the midnight sky when he reached the Royd Haggard ranch; the place was dark and asleep. He rode to the front of the main house at a slow walk, dropped the reins of the two horses over the porch rail of the house, and backed the Ovaro away. He walked the pinto away as he left the two still figures in front of the silent house, a grim gift for Royd Haggard when he woke in the morning.

Fargo had the Ovaro pick its way through the trees. Ellen's place was closest and he hoped he could reach it as searing pain consumed his entire body and he fought off the increasing waves of weakness. The blood from his temple had caked along the side of his face and his shirt was sticky where it pressed against his right side. He stayed in the saddle only by sheer determination, pulling himself back each time he swayed from side to side. Finally he leaned forward, his head pressed against the thick neck of the pinto. The moon was nearing the horizon line when the horse stepped to the front of Ellen's house and Fargo half-slid, half-fell from the saddle. He pulled himself forward, fell against the front door, and leaned against it as he pounded with the side of his fist.

He heard her footsteps after a moment and hoarseness

of his own voice. "It's me, Fargo," he said, and called out again. She slid the latch bolt back and the door opened and Ellen raised the kerosene lamp she held in one hand, her eyes widening as she stared at him.

"My God," she breathed, and reached out to him as he swayed and stepped into the house. "This way," she said, and led him through the living room and into a bedroom where he saw the wide bed, the sheet pulled back. She guided him to the edge of the bed and he sank down into its softness, his face pressed against the pillow. "Don't move. I'll be right back," Ellen said, and he heard her hurry away. He closed his eyes and pulled them open as Ellen returned. She wore a dark-blue bathrobe, he noticed for the first time, the neckline dipping low as she bent over. He glimpsed the edge of one long breast as she began to pull his clothes off. She left only the bottoms of his underdrawers on and he felt the night air cool against the burning of his body.

"What happened?" Ellen asked as she used cotton wads to gently wipe the blood from his face and ribs.

"Royd Haggard sent a message," Fargo told her. "I sent him an answer."

"Then it's him, he's the one," Ellen said.

"Didn't say that," Fargo answered.

She accepted the answer without further comment and poured a smooth salve from a crock and began to message his body with it. "Comfrey and wintergreen compress," she said. "Marvelous for bruises and muscle aches." The salve did indeed feel good, but the soothing touch of her hands felt even better. She rubbed the back of his neck, down across his shoulder blades, and along the muscled firmness of his sore back. He turned over at her request and she rubbed more salve across his chest and down his legs. He watched the loveliness of her face as she concentrated on her ministering and saw her tongue come out to lick the dryness from her lips as she massaged his flat abdomen, moved lower, and quickly drew away. She shifted position and he caught the fullness of one breast as the robe parted for an instant.

Her strong yet gentle massaging and the action of the salve acted as a narcotic and he felt his eyes closing. He lay still, enjoying the wonderfulness of her touch, until he finally slid into a deep sleep. The last thing he remembered was Ellen's hands smooth against him and then something soft against his cheek for the briefest of moments. He slept the deep sleep of the exhausted, and when he woke, the room was flooded with sunlight. He lay still awhile longer and carefully began to flex his muscles. There was still pain but only an echo of what he had felt when he arrived at Ellen's place. Her salve was indeed made of healing properties. Even the back of his neck was now only a dull throb.

The flood of sunlight in the room told him it had to be at least midmorning and he was about to swing out of bed when he heard the sound of a carriage drawing to a stop outside. He heard the front door of the house open and then Ellen's voice. "What brings you this way?" he heard her ask.

"Have you seen Fargo?" the question came back on Alicia's voice, and Fargo's brows lifted. He waited, listening as Ellen paused before answering. "Saw him yesterday morning," Ellen said.

"I mean since then, such as last night," Alicia asked, a trace of impatience in her tone.

"No. Why?" Ellen answered evenly and Fargo felt the smile come to his lips.

"He was in a vicious fight at the Clay Springs Playhouse last night. Two of my hands were there and they told me about it this morning," Alicia said. "He was hurt and I'm wondering what happened to him."

"He probably went off into the hills somewhere. That'd be like him," Ellen said.

"If you see him tell him to come by my place," Alicia said, and again Fargo heard the combination of impatience and authoritativeness in her tone with Ellen. He lay still and listened to the carriage drive away. He waited, arms stretched behind his head, and Ellen came into the room only moments later.

"You're awake," she said, her eyes moving quickly across his smoothly muscled body. "Did you hear?"

"Yes. Why didn't you tell her I was here?" he asked.

Ellen shrugged. "Just didn't," she said.

"How about a real answer?" Fargo smiled and watched the stubbornness come into Ellen's face.

"I don't think she has to know everything," she said.

"That's better, but it's still not the truth," Fargo said, holding the slightly chiding smile. "You didn't tell her because you were sure she'd conclude the same thing you would've if you'd found me at her place." Ellen frowned back, her lips tight. "And it's likely you were wrong. Alicia's wiser than you think."

"She'd have assumed it, I know it," Ellen snapped.

"How come she didn't see the Ovaro?" Fargo asked.

"I put him in the barn last night," she said. "How do you feel?" she asked, dismissing further talk of Alicia.

"Much better. Almost myself," Fargo said.

"There's a hot tub drawn and waiting in the next room. I'll be in the kitchen when you're finished," she said, and hurried out as he started to swing from the bed.

The hot tub was another welcome embrace and he

let himself soak in the warmth of the water. When he finished, he dressed and found his bloodstained shirt cleaned and ironed and hanging on the back of a chair. He put it on and went into the kitchen, where Ellen wore a small white apron over her Levi's and dark-green shirt.

She dished out sweetcakes and sausage with hot coffee as he sat down at the table. After she'd set the coffeepot down and passed close, his arms curled around her waist and he pulled her to him. His mouth came down on hers, gently, and it took a moment for her lips to grow soft. He pulled back. Ellen wasn't the kind for being rushed, he was certain. "For all your good nursing," he said.

"A simple thank-you would have done," she said as she sat down across from him.

"I like my way better," he said, and he saw her hold back a smile.

"I'm glad I could help," she said. "What now?"

"There's a lot more to find out before I go deciding anything," Fargo said.

"Even after last night?" Ellen queried.

"Even after last night," he echoed.

She shrugged and fell silent as he finished the meal. Then she walked to the barn with him, waiting while he saddled the pinto. He turned to her when he finished. "When will you be back?" she asked.

It was his turn to shrug. "When I've more to tell," he said. "It was real nice last night."

"It was nice doing it," Ellen said. "But that's a hard way to get a back rub."

"I was careless. I let myself be taken off-guard. I didn't expect Royd Haggard would pick a bar as his place to answer," Fargo said. His hand came up to press against her waist, but she stayed stiff and he moved away and swung onto the horse. She watched him leave from the barn.

He took the nearest low hill and stayed at a slow pace as his body protested anything faster. He had crossed the slope of the hill and turned along a ridge when he spotted the riders, six of them, with Royd Haggard's authoritative figure unmistakable among them. He could have avoided them, but he decided not to and held his place as they came toward him. He had the big Sharps in the crook of his arm as Royd Haggard rode to a halt. He saw the man eye the rifle.

"Goddamn you, Fargo, you didn't have to kill them," Royd Haggard boomed.

"They didn't give me much choice," Fargo said.

"You keep on accusing me and I might send more," the man threatened.

"Expect them back the same way," Fargo answered.

"You've no right to go around accusing anyone."

"I didn't accuse you yet."

"You as much as did."

"As much as isn't accusing."

"You think you're a hard piece," Haggard roared.

"Hard enough. I'm after the truth. I'll get it," Fargo said.

"Not over my good name," the man said.

"Over whatever it takes," Fargo returned with icy steadiness.

Royd Haggard threw him another hard glare before he wheeled his horse around and led his men away.

Fargo kept the rifle raised till he was out of sight and slowly moved the pinto down the next slope after returning the Sharps to its saddle holster. He let thoughts revolve through his mind as he rode. Haggard's men hadn't followed orders. He was convinced of that. Haggard had wanted him out of the way, but beaten to a pulp, not killed. Perhaps he'd decided that would be just as effective and smarter. Or perhaps that fact meant something very different. Fargo pondered the questions. Little things still nagged, refused to fit, just as Royd Haggard didn't completely fit. But the man had to stay a prime suspect.

Amos Dillon swam into Fargo's thoughts. The recluse had been too nervous when Ellen questioned him. He knew something more about Tom Johnson than the turn-away answers he had given. But what? In any case, Amos Dillon came next, before Zach Traynor or Billy Harrison, Fargo decided. He turned the pinto southward along the edge of the Smokey Hills and it was near dusk when he reached the base of the section Ellen had shown him. He began to climb into the hills as night pressed its dark blanket over the land. He continued on under a filtered moon until he finally halted to bed down under a red cedar. He had gone far enough. Morning would find him in the middle hills and he'd go carefully from there.

Amos Dillon was a recluse who had successfully hidden away for damn near a lifetime. Others had tried to find him, Fargo was certain, right up to the present moment. Some no doubt out of curiosity, some just for fun, and some probably thought the old recluse had gold hidden away with him. Then the very recent ones had searched for their own reasons, whatever they turned out to be. But they had all failed because none had been trailsmen. They tried to find the tracks of a man who knew how to leave no tracks. They hunted caves in hills honeycombed with caves and came up empty-handed. They looked for Amos Dillon without knowing how to look for him. Fargo smiled as he closed his eyes. He'd not make those mistakes. Experience and acquired wisdoms would prevent that. He slid into sleep, wrapped in the blanket of the night.

Morning brought the sun and he woke, used his canteen to wash, and led the Ovaro into a thicket where the horse quickly became all but invisible. Fargo's eyes swept the hills. He was almost at the place where Ellen had met with Amos Dillon. He retrieved the Ovaro, stayed in the thick tree cover, and moved forward on foot. Finally, halting, he sank down to one knee. He had reached the spot where the recluse had showed himself to Ellen. He saw the wide bed of spotted winter-green with their mottled green-and-white leaves and pure white flowers and, to the left side of the nearest hill, the line of blue-velvet irises. He had marked both in his mind during that first meeting and his eyes moved across the terrain. Amos Dillon did not live here. He had watched them and come down to meet them, but he did not live here.

The recluse lived in a cave, Fargo felt certain of that, a place he dwelled all the year through. Such a place had to have certain requirements. Such a place would not be far from water. And not just a trickling stream. Water that could offer sustenance and bring game. And Amos Dillon would not choose a place where he had to travel far to reach that water. That was important, especially in the bitter months of winter. The requirements stayed in his mind as Fargo's eyes searched the distant hills. He rose and led the Ovaro on foot, staying in the dense tree cover as he continued to scan the hills. Suddenly he halted. A flash of blue caught his eye, higher into the hills, sunlight on water, a small lake all but hidden away.

Fargo stayed in the thick trees as he moved toward the water. The water took shape, became a circular pond undoubtedly spring-fed. He gave the Ovaro a long and loose tether on a low branch and went forward alone. The pond lay almost in the center of the four slopes, and as he drew closer, he saw a sizable stream that spilled from one end to wander down the slope. He caught the flash of a brook trout as it leapt into the air.

Fargo settled down in a heavy thicket of mountain brush and let his gaze move across the three slopes that faced him. The north one was too steep. Amos Dillon's cave would not be there. Carrying water up in the winter would be a virtual impossibility. The west slope stretched out too far. That left the east slope, and the one he was on.

The east slope was closest of all to the pond and its rise the least steep. Amos's cave was somewhere on the east slope, Fargo felt certain. He peered along the terrain covered with box elder, black walnut, and shagbark hickory, a green wall impenetrable to the eye. He sank back against a tree trunk and settled down. He'd stay in the thicket. To come out would be to risk being seen by Amos.

If that happened, the recluse would vanish. These hills were his home and he'd have a dozen alternate places to disappear into. This was the time for waiting, and waiting, as every wild-creature hunter knew, was but another form of action. Fargo kept his gaze on the circular pond as the morning moved into the afternoon and the afternoon shadows began to slowly lengthen. A porcupine visited the pond, along with two gray foxes and a small cluster of white-tailed deer. A flight of Baltimore orioles, along with purple grackles and the ever-present yellow-breasted meadowlarks landed to pick along the sago pondweeds at the edge of the water.

But Amos Dillon did not appear. It was likely he had come and gone in the early dawn, Fargo realized, and took his eyes from the pond to scour the slope. If Amos moved through the hillside, he was doing so with the practiced skill that left every leaf unmoved. Fargo smiled in silence admiration and returned his gaze to the pond. The sun moved across the sky until it began to slip behind the high hills and the ground shadows lengthened further to become a gray blanket. The songbirds winged away and he spied an opossum come to the pond, first of the night hunters out for an early drink. He watched as the opossum moved on and suddenly caught a movement in the trees that bordered the left side of the pond.

He sat up, every part of him instantly alert, and a few moments later he saw the figure move from the trees. Amos Dillon carried his rifle in one hand, a water bucket in the other. Fargo rose and drew the Colt as the recluse moved to the edge of the pond. Amos would have to put down the rifle to fill the water bucket and Fargo crept forward as he took aim. He halted at the edge of the underbrush, waited, watched Amos Dillon finally lay the rifle down and lean forward with both arms outstretched as he filled the bucket with the clear pond water. Fargo aimed carefully as his finger tightened on the trigger. The single shot exploded to send a shower of dirt into the air a fraction of an inch from Amos' left leg.

The recluse dropped the bucket, spun on his knees, and started to reach for the rifle. Fargo's second shot slammed into the ground just in front of Amos' hand, and the man yanked his arm back. "Don't try it again," Fargo called as he stepped from the thicket and marched toward the pond, the Colt raised and ready to fire. Astonishment flooded Amos Dillon's face as he saw the big man come toward him.

"You're the one that was with Ellen?" He frowned.

"That's right," Fargo said as the old recluse stared back with a kind of disbelief in his pale-blue eyes.

"You're something special, mister. Nobody's ever come close to finding me all these years," Amos said.

"Get your bucket before it floats away from you," Fargo said, and the man turned, reached out, and hauled the filled bucket onto the shore as Fargo picked up the rifle. "I came to talk," Fargo said.

"We can talk here," the recluse said.

"It'll be dark in minutes," Fargo said.

The recluse nodded and began to move up the slope with his bucket. Fargo followed and emptied the shells from the rifle as he climbed. Amos Dillon snaked his way through thick tree cover, mostly shagbark hickory, and the darkness bore down quickly but Fargo stayed on his heels. Finally, the man pushed through what seemed a wall of foliage and Fargo saw the cave appear. He entered with Amos and found himself in an empty, wide cave and the man caught his frown. Amos Dillon stepped deeper into the cave, pressed a hand against the back wall and a section of stone pushed open.

A shaft of light burst out as Amos stepped into the cave hidden behind the first one, and Fargo, following, saw the three kerosene lamps that lighted the cave. A mattress lay against one wall and Fargo saw a rocking chair, clothes in neat stacks, trapping gear along another wall, and a stack of old journals and books. A fireplace area walled with stone took up one corner of the cave and a low-legged table, plainly hand-carved, stood beside two bamboo mats that lay across the floor. It was little wonder that the man had stayed a recluse all the years. His cave was well-hidden, secure, and he knew how to live a self-sufficient life.

But Tom Johnson had visited him through all the years. There had to be a reason beyond the need to talk about old times. "You were holding back when Ellen questioned you. Why?" Fargo said as the man set the water bucket down.

"I wasn't holding back. I was upset at the news she brought," Amos answered.

Fargo allowed a smile. "Don't play games with me. Tom Johnson made regular visits to you for at least twenty years. Ellen just accepted that as part of her growing up. Alicia doesn't know why. I'm sure the first Mrs. Johnson knew, but she's not around. That leaves you. I want answers."

"I gave you answers when you came with Ellen," the recluse insisted, and Fargo's tone hardened.

"Bullshit answers. What was it between you and Tom Johnson? What kept him coming up here all those years? What made him look after you?" Fargo questioned.

"Nothing that concerns the killings," Amos Dillon said. The old man was being stubborn and Fargo swore silently. He didn't want to use force to get answers and he turned Amos' reply in his mind. The question spiraled from inside him.

"Something that concerned Ellen?" he speared, and Amos Dillon wasn't quick enough to keep the startled, almost frightened expression from his face. Bull's-eye, Fargo snorted silently. He hit paydirt. "Talk, dammit. What was it? How did Ellen figure into it?" he roared. "Don't make me get it out of you the hard way, Amos."

The recluse peered at him, but the stubbornness had gone from his face, Fargo saw, and he seemed suddenly little more than a tired old man. "Tom dead, after all these years, and killed the way it happened. It's all I've thought about since you and Ellen were here," Amos said as he sank into the rocking chair. "We had a secret, Tom and I. I didn't break it when he was alive. I'm not for breaking it now just because he's dead."

"It might help me catch whoever had him killed. You'd want that, wouldn't you?" Fargo countered.

Amos frowned for a long moment and then his words came slowly, painfully. "I don't see how it'd help you any," he murmured. "But then, you never know," he added in self-reflection.

"It might, if it concerns Ellen," Fargo pressed, and the old recluse's shrug was the gesture of a man too tired to know what was right any longer.

"All right," he murmured. "All right, I'll tell you."

6

"Tom wasn't Ellen's real father," Amos Dillon said, and Fargo felt his brows lift. "But he'd always loved Ellen's mother, Donna. When the real father up and disappeared, Tom offered to marry Donna and say he was the baby's father. Donna, scared and ashamed of becoming a marked woman, took him up on the offer. Tom Johnson was a fine man and Donna came to appreciate that all the rest of her life."

"How did you figure into this?" Fargo asked.

"First, Ellen's real father was my cousin, Zeb. He was never any damn good, except when it came to getting girls in trouble. When he ran off, I felt kind of responsible for what he'd done, knowing he'd never show up again. But I was the only one who knew he was the baby's real father except Tom and Donna. Tom and I agreed it was a secret we'd keep forever."

"Why did you stay around all these years, up here in the hills?" Fargo questioned.

"Tom was just starting out to build his ranch. He used to go away on long cattle drives. He asked me to be near for Donna, in case she needed help. But I never liked town living, and besides, there were folks around then who knew I was Zeb's cousin. We decided

101

we didn't want to risk questions, gossip, or tongue-wagging rumor."

"So you stayed in the hills," Fargo supplied, and the recluse nodded.

"For the early years I stayed in the hills and came down at night to check on Donna. She was the only one who knew where I was in the hills besides Tom. Finally, Tom grew rich and I grew to like living alone in the hills. It became best for all of us and Tom would come to visit at least once a month. Sometimes he'd bring things I could use, sometimes we'd just talk. When Donna died, his visits were a kind of trip into memories for him. Then he got married again and he didn't come as often as he used to."

"I heard Alicia never liked his going off to meet you. I think she could never understand it," Fargo said.

"No matter, not anymore," Amos said as he rose from the rocking chair and took in a deep breath. "I told you it wouldn't help you any with the killings," he said.

"You were right. I can't see where it has any connection," Fargo agreed.

"There's nothing but hurt to come out of it if you tell Ellen," Amos said.

"Agreed. I won't be telling her anything. Tom Johnson was her father in what's maybe the only real and important way. I'll not be changing that for Ellen or him," Fargo said.

"Thanks," Amos Dillon said simply.

"What are you going to do now?" Fargo asked.

"Don't know. Now there won't even be Tom's visits anymore. It's all changed. I might move on, find me another mountain somewhere," the old recluse said.

"Anything else you can tell me? Anything Tom

Johnson said to you about problems?'' Fargo asked.

"He told me about maybe going to have an operation, but nothing else. That's the truth. After what I just told you there'd be no point in holding back anything else," Amos said.

Fargo nodded, satisfied with the answer. "I'll be going back now," he said.

"If I leave, it won't be right away. I'd like knowing if you find out the truth about what happened," Amos said.

"I'll come tell you," Fargo promised, and Amos Dillon walked to the opening of the outer cave with him and watched him start down the slope in the darkness. The moon had come up to afford a pale light, and after two wrong turns, he found the spot where he'd left the Ovaro. He rode slowly down the slope.

The visit to Amos Dillon had answered his misgivings but had left him feeling slightly soiled, as though he'd pried into places he'd no right to pry. But he could eliminate past ghosts now. The murders at Doc Schubert's had a very real and present motive.

He put away further speculation as he reached the base of the hills and turned south toward Clay Springs. When he reached the saloon, he tethered the horse and strode inside. He caught the flash of surprise in the bartender's eyes as the man saw him enter. "Relax, friend. I don't expect any more trouble tonight," Fargo said blandly.

"That was some battle you put up," the bartender said.

"Had no choice," Fargo said. "Haven't changed my mind about anything, either. But I'm not staying tonight," he said as he turned and walked to the far end of the bar where the woman with the brassy blond curls still sat atop the high stool. She watched him approach, a veiled amusement over her eyes. "Came by to say thanks," he said.

"Wasn't taking sides. I just don't like seeing a man bushwhacked," the woman said.

"I had a chance because of your pitcher of cold water. I owe you," Fargo said. "You've a name?"

"Goldie," the woman said.

"Maybe you and I ought to talk some, Goldie," Fargo said. "Maybe you've heard things to help me."

"Sorry. I don't listen to gossip and I don't repeat it," the woman said. "I take care of my girls. That's enough."

Fargo smiled. The woman was a survivor who played a careful game of survival, and he couldn't blame her. "Thanks again," he said. She nodded and he wondered if anything ever changed that careful mask she wore.

He walked from the saloon and, once outside, headed the pinto to Alicia's home. She was awake, heard him arrive, and had the door open before he swung from the saddle. Her arms were around him at once, the warm breasts pressing against him through the thin silk of a pink nightgown.

"I've been so worried about you. I heard what happened at the saloon," Alicia murmured as she led him into the house.

"I'm all right," he told her.

"Where've you been?"

"Resting up in the hills."

"Why didn't you come to me?" Alicia asked. He had expected the question.

"Didn't know if I might be followed," he said. "I didn't want to bring more trouble to your doorstep."

She accepted the answer with another kiss. "Can you

stay tonight?'' she asked, and he nodded and she led him into the bedroom. ''I guess there's no doubt now that Royd Haggard is the man you want,'' she said as he sank onto the edge of the bed with her.

''Maybe,'' he said.

''Maybe?'' Alicia frowned. ''He just tried to have you killed. Isn't that enough proof?''

''No, not yet,'' Fargo said. ''Things don't fit right yet.''

Alicia's frown stayed as she studied his face. ''Such as?'' she queried.

''Little things. I'm not sure of anything yet,'' he said. ''I went to see Amos Dillon.''

Her eyes widened in surprise. ''You found him?''

''I found him,'' Fargo said.

''I'm amazed. Absolutely amazed,'' Alicia said. ''What'd you find out from him?''

''Nothing of any help. He talked about old times with Tom. I'm convinced he doesn't know anything about the killings or who or what was behind them,'' Fargo said.

''Then I guess we can write him off,'' Alicia said, and her fingers began to unbutton his shirt. ''Maybe we should write the whole thing off.''

''And not know who had Doc Schubert and your husband killed?'' Fargo inquired.

''I want to know, but not at the expense of something happening to you. I want you here with me,'' she said, slipping the shirt from him and her hands moving across his chest. ''I'd like to convince you to stay.''

''I can't stop you from trying,'' Fargo said, and Alicia's smile came against his mouth. She wriggled her shoulders and the nightgown fell away and her deep breasts were against him as his hands curled around each. In moments he was naked beside her, and her full-fleshed body was straining against his, thighs opening for him and her deep cries rising at once. She hugged his face to her breasts, luscious smothering, as her hands sought him, held, and caressed. She pulled him into her with a scream of pure pleasure.

The curve of her belly jiggled against him as he lay atop her, his movements held back, slowness despite her gasping, anxious hurry. He luxuriated in the almost-encompassing fullness of her. Alicia cried out, half-laughed, reveled in the thrustings of him with earthy abandon, no sensitive delicacy in her pleasures but a headlong embrace of the flesh. "Oh Jesus, oh, oh . . . oh, Jesus," Alicia gasped as that moment spiraled up inside her and her climax exploded in a groaning and quivering. She clasped him to her until, with a deep groan, she fell back on the bed.

She pulled Fargo with her, held him atop her as she drew in deep breaths and her full-fleshed thighs stayed wrapped around him. Finally, she let her legs fall away and he slid down beside her, where she cradled his head against her deep breasts. "How was that for convincing?" she asked.

"It was a damn good try."

"Meaning I'll have to keep trying?"

"Something like that," Fargo said, and she chuckled and kept his head against her breasts. He lay still, listened to her fall asleep. Her arms around him grew limp and he shifted and lay on his back. He stayed awake a spell as he made plans for the coming day until he finally embraced sleep himself.

When morning came, Alicia was still hard asleep as

he slipped from the bed, pulled on trousers, and went outside, where he washed at the well. She was still asleep when he returned for the rest of his clothes and left with a last glance back at the full-figured beauty of her. He rode away, paused at a stand of blackberries, and breakfasted. Then he turned his horse toward the Hart ranch. The morning would be another exercise in triggering a reaction, a slightly different approach this time. But it was the only quick way to lean the base things he had to know. When he reached the ranch, his sweeping glance did not find Zach Traynor.

"He's in the stable," one of the ranch hands said at Fargo's question. "It's his day off." Fargo nodded back and rode to the opened double doors of the stable, where he saw Zach Traynor had just saddled a brown gelding. Fargo dismounted and the man's face darkened at once as he saw his visitor.

"I told you to stay away from me," the man growled.

"I think you ought to know something. You're looking more and more like the man I'm after," Fargo said.

"You're crazy," Traynor shot back.

"You hated Tom Johnson for firing you and calling you what you are, a damn thief," Fargo said. "After he fired you, you had time to hire those three killers, and most important, you knew Tom Johnson was going to have the operation. You were still working there when he decided that."

"I wasn't the only one who knew that," Traynor protested.

"No, but you threatened to kill him and you had the time, the chance, and the reason to put it into action," Fargo said.

"You've no goddamn proof of anything," Traynor shouted.

"Give me another few days," Fargo said. "Unless you want to draw on me now."

Zach Traynor's mouth quivered. "No, no, I heard you were real fast. But I'm not letting you hang this on me, you can be damn sure of that," the man said.

"When I'm ready, I'll hang it on whoever should get it. Meanwhile, I'm giving you a chance to own up. That might get you some jail time instead of hanging," Fargo said.

"You won't be hanging me, Fargo," Traynor snarled.

"Your choice," Fargo said. "I'll be back." Traynor spit silent curses through his eyes as Fargo turned, walked from the stable, and rode away with confident deliberateness. He knew the man watched him move along the open road and turn up into the first slope of the low hills. He could feel the man's eyes burning into his back with fury and fear.

Fargo moved slowly up the slope, stayed in open land until he was more than halfway up the hill. Then he turned into the trees that dotted the slope—hackberry and black oak with some red cedar. He halted, waited, and peered out from inside the trees. It was only a few minutes when he glimpsed the horse and rider dart into the trees below and to his right.

He waited, then continued to move slowly across the slope, his wild-creature hearing tuned to the sounds from behind and to his right. It was only another few minutes when he picked up the crack of a horse stepping on a twig, then the dry rustle of underbrush being pushed back. Fargo let himself move in and out of the trees, aware that his pursuer would spot him each time he went into the open. He moved into still another stand of trees, aware that the rider following had come close now. He moved into a thick cluster of black oak, but this time he halted and dropped noiselessly to the ground. He moved the Ovaro into the deepest part of the trees and then stepped forward in a crouch.

The horse and rider came into view, moving carefully through the trees. Fargo saw that Zach Traynor had a five-shot double-action Remington-Rider revolver in his hand. Fargo drew his Colt, took careful aim, and fired. The pistol flew from Zach Traynor's hand and the man fell from the saddle as the horse bolted. Fargo stepped forward as Zach Traynor pushed to his feet. "Bushwhacking's a coward's way," he commented almost casually.

"Goddamn you, go ahead and shoot, then," Traynor shouted. "You say you think it was me. Now's your chance. Go ahead and kill me."

"Need more proof. I don't kill a man till I'm sure I'm right about him," Fargo said.

"Goddamn you," Zach Traynor exploded, and flung himself forward in a lunging dive. "You're not going to hang me for this," he shouted.

Fargo brought the barrel of the Colt down in a sharp arc. It smashed into Zach Traynor's skull and the man pitched facedown, unconscious. Fargo used his foot to turn him over and his eyes traveled over the man's run-down boots, the cracked leather of his gun belt, the torn place on his holster, his Levi's with at least two patches.

He turned away after a moment and swung onto his horse. He heard Zach Traynor regaining consciousness as he rode away. Traynor would hold his anger, nurture his hate, but he'd return to his job. He'd wait and be on guard, silently plotting a possible next move. That was his nature, a small-minded man that could be goaded into stupid moves out of desperation. Lunging into the barrel of a six-gun had been an example. He was a weasel, but weasels could be dangerous. They struck in the night, in cunning and stealth. Zach Traynor had to remain a suspect, but there were things about him that didn't fit right, either, and Fargo grimaced as he moved the Ovaro across the sloping terrain. So far everyone fit and yet didn't fit quite right.

He found a spot to rest and decided to nap the remainder of the day away. He sure hadn't gotten a full night's sleep. Alicia had seen to that. Besides, he had to wait for the deep of night for his next visit. He lay down and fitfully slept until darkness. He woke and used a strip of beef jerky from his saddlebag for a meal and topped it with a cluster of blueberries he found. He moved from the slope and made a small detour to reach Ellen's place. The house was dark but he knocked and in a few moments he heard the latch bolt slide back and Ellen opened the door. No rifle in her hand this time, but she had a firm grip on a big Savage and North double-action revolver with a ring trigger.

"It's just me," he said, and she lowered the gun.

"Didn't expect a visit. I was tired and went to bed early," Ellen said, and drew the robe tighter around herself. It pressed against her breasts and hips and he saw no sign of a nightgown underneath.

"I've a question about Zach Traynor. Your pa fired him for stealing over the years. Did he make Zach give the money back?" Fargo asked.

"There was none to give back. Zach Traynor lost whatever he stole on gambling and drinking," Ellen said.

Fargo nodded, the answer falling into place in his

mind. "See you tomorrow maybe," he said. "By the way, I talked with Amos Dillon." Ellen's eyes widened in surprise. "He was surprised, too," Fargo said dryly.

"Why'd you go back to talk to Amos?" she asked.

"I wasn't satisfied with the answers last time."

"And now?"

"I'm satisfied," he said. "He may go away from here," he said.

"That doesn't surprise me," Ellen said. "He have anything else to tell you?"

"No, nothing else," Fargo said.

"Where are you going now?"

"Why?"

"I wondered if you wanted a place to bed down," she said.

"Is that an invitation?" he said, laughing, and she gave a half-shrug.

"Alicia's not the only one who can play hostess," Ellen sniffed. "Only my invitations have limits on them."

"Of course." Fargo grinned and drew a quick glare. "Some other time, maybe. I'm on my way to find Billy Harrison," he said.

She stepped closer, concern in her face at once. "Be careful. I hear he's very fast with a gun," she said.

"Thanks for the warning. Now you go back to sleep," he said.

"Fat chance," Ellen snorted. "Now I'll be waiting and worrying."

He cupped her chin in his hand. "It's nice to be worried over," he said.

"It was general worrying, not personal," she said quickly.

He laughed as he drew his hand from her chin. "Of

111

course," he said, and drew the glare again. "I'll stop by soon as I can." He waited till he heard the latch bolt click into place. He sent the Ovaro into a fast trot, climbed the low rolling ground, and moved into the higher terrain as he made his way to Ridge Hill. He knew the way very well now, on this his third visit.

The moon had started its curving path down the far reaches of the sky when he drew up near the shack. This was the time Billy Harrison returned, in the deep of night, to eat and change clothes and flee before daybreak. Only this time it would be different.

The kerosene lamp that seemed to stay on all the time still lighted the shack Fargo saw as he slid from the saddle to move forward on foot. He halted at the edge of the open land near the shack, the Colt in hand, but he neither saw nor heard anything. Dammit, he swore, his eyes narrowed. Was he too late? Had Billy Harrison come and gone already? If so, he'd start his vigil at dusk tomorrow, Fargo swore at himself and listened again. When he heard nothing, he darted forward in a crouch and burst into the shack, the Colt raised, his finger on the trigger. He found himself staring at the empty room. But Billy Harrison had been there, he saw bitterly. Fresh plates on the table with leftover food still warm and a new pile of dirty shirts. Fargo swore again as he thrust the Colt back into its holster and strode from the shack.

He'd taken but two steps outside when he saw the smallish, slender figure with the Remington-Beals six-gun pointed at him. Fargo halted and swore silently. He'd let himself be tricked. Behind the revolver he saw a clean-shaven, very youthful face, handsome in a boyish way, almost innocent in appearance. Only the eyes betrayed the rest of the face. They were dark and glittery and held danger, not innocence, in their depths.

"End of the road, big man." Billy Harrison smiled.

"It was you, then," Fargo tossed back.

"I didn't say that," Billy Harrison snapped.

"This is as much as saying so," Fargo snapped.

"Hell it is," the younger man threw back.

"He broke you up with Ellen. You were angling to marry her, had her wrapped around your thumb. You'd have fallen into real money and he did you out of it," Fargo said.

"So he did, the old bastard," Billy Harrison admitted.

"And you hated him for it."

"That's right."

"You're wanted for killing three men in New Mexico Territory. One more wouldn't bother you any," Fargo said.

"That's right. But I didn't have him killed. I wanted that pleasure for myself. I gave the others a fair chance to draw on me. I'd have done the same for him," Billy Harrison said.

Fargo turned the youth's words in his mind. They had a note of bragging in them and his eyes went to the revolver trained on him. "Yes, you'd have let him try to draw on you. You fancy yourself as a gunfighter," Fargo said, and saw the youth's eyes narrow.

"There's three dead men that'll prove that," Billy Harrison said.

"Sitting ducks probably," Fargo sniffed disdainfully and the youth's face hardened.

"You sayin' I can't outshoot anybody?" Billy Harrison frowned.

"That's right," Fargo said.

"You'd like me to let you draw on me, wouldn't you?" Harrison said, caution coming into his voice.

"Not really," Fargo said, and the younger man

113

frowned. Fargo smiled inwardly. He'd put Billy Harrison off-balance now. "I wouldn't want to kill you yet, not till I've proof you did it," he said.

"Kill me? Shit, you're afraid for your own hide," Billy Harrison sneered.

Fargo kept his face expressionless. The youth needed a little more push. "You're good with words, I'll give you that," he said.

Billy Harrison's face darkened. "You son of a bitch. Let's see if you've got any guts," he snarled, and thrust the Remington into his holster. Fargo smiled inwardly. The youth was angry and excited; he wanted to prove himself. He'd grab at his gun and let excitement destroy the smooth movement essential to a smooth and accurate draw. "You call," Billy Harrison snapped out brazenly. Conceit leading him into another mistake, Fargo smiled inwardly. But he waited. He wanted a little more insurance. He didn't want to kill Billy Harrison. He hadn't lied about that. He hadn't proof enough for that, not yet.

He let another ten seconds count off and saw Billy Harrison's hand twitch and tighten. Fargo held another two seconds. Billy Harrison had already lost rhythm. "Now," Fargo barked. The Colt was in his hand and firing while Billy Harrison was just bringing his gun up. The bullet cut across the top of the youth's hand, and he cursed in pain as he dropped the gun. His eyes held fury, surprise, and a touch of sudden fear as he backed away. "No near miss, sonny. I could've killed you," Fargo said. "But I told you I'm not ready for that."

Billy Harrison backed away again and Fargo dropped the Colt into its holster. He expected the youth to halt and grow a little less fearful, but suddenly Billy Harrison

114

flung himself sideways into a nearby thicket of high brush. His hand came up out of the brush and Fargo caught the glint of moonlight on metal. He threw himself sideways as the shot whistled past his head, hit the ground, and rolled as another shot threw up a spray of soil at his heels. Damn Harrison, Fargo cursed. He'd had a second gun inside his shirt. He kept rolling as he drew the Colt and heard Harrison running into the darkness. The next sound that came was the galloping of hooves racing into the night.

He grimaced as he pushed to his feet. Billy Harrison had reached the first ridge and was racing into the night. Fargo holstered the Colt and walked to where he had left the Ovaro.

Billy Harrison revolved in his mind as he slowly rode through the trees. The youth wouldn't disappear. He wouldn't flee. He was too conceited for that. He'd hole up somewhere, or maybe continue doing odd jobs at local ranches. But he'd wait for another chance to prove his gunfighting prowess. That was something he had to do if he were the guilty one, and he'd do it if he weren't guilty. He'd have to stay close enough to hear what developed.

But Billy Harrison couldn't be dismissed. He had motive, the ability to carry through, and the opportunity to do so. But once again, as with Haggard and Zach Traynor, there were things about Billy Harrison that didn't quite fit. Little things, Fargo admitted. Unimportant little things? he wondered. Or were they meaningful? Was he letting little things assume too much importance? The thought stuck for a moment. Or was he simply missing something important about one of the three? He had no answer for the questions, but there was more than what he had found, something else he couldn't pin down yet. But it was there, the evidence that would mark the real killer of Doc Schubert and the others. He felt not unlike a man who knows there is gold in front of him and can't see it.

He was still wrestling with his thoughts as he watched the dawn come up. He rode higher into the hills. A wide-branched red oak beckoned and he halted in its shade, undressed to his underdrawers, and stretched out on his bedroll. There'd be time to speculate further, he knew, time to find the pieces that still eluded him, the pieces that would pinpoint the real killer of Doc Schubert and the others. He closed his eyes and let sleep come to him.

7

The sun was in midafternoon when he woke. He made his way from the low hills after a visit to a nearby spring and rode south toward Royd Haggard's place. He circled when he neared the Haggard spread, found a thick cluster of oak from which he could watch the ranch and not be seen. Staying in the saddle, Fargo watched Royd Haggard as the man moved around his ranch, talking to his foreman, checking on a lame horse. He watched the man ride out to look at a herd of uncorralled steers and finally return to supervise other activities at the ranch. He watched from his hidden vantage place for over an hour and finally backed the Ovaro out of the trees and rode away.

He turned toward the smaller ranch that was Ben Hart's, climbed a hillock that let him view the modest spread, and quickly found Zach Traynor. He watched as Traynor helped in training a half-dozen unbroken mounts with the aid of three other ranch hands, continued to peer at the man as he went on with other chores. He watched Zach Traynor for almost an hour, and as night descended and the ranch hands made for the bunkhouse, he turned away and rode on. He rode across the hills to Billy Harrison's shack. The youth wouldn't be there, he knew, but he approached cautiously and finally stepped into the empty shack. He stood in the center of the room, his eyes half-closed, and let the smell and feel of Billy Harrison flow around him. Finally he turned from the shack, climbed back onto the Ovaro, and rode away.

He thought about waiting till the night was deep to see if Harrison returned. It was more than likely he would. But Fargo pushed away the thought. He didn't want another face-off with the youth, not yet. It wouldn't provide him with what he needed and he might end up having to kill Billy Harrison. He didn't want that, either, not till he was sure. He rode slowly through the moonlight, letting his thoughts float freely of themselves. Billy Harrison, Royd Haggard, Zach Traynor, their faces swam in front of him. He had watched the last two with his mind swept clean, his senses pushed almost to blankness. He had watched each man to see if something came to him to trigger thoughts, if locking into the feel of Haggard and Traynor would bring some transmission of senses that might define the undefined. He had done the same standing in Billy Harrison's shack.

It was a practice the Navajo shaman used, to absorb the spirit and essence of another being, a joining together with that spirit and essence. Sometimes it brought remarkable results. He had been witness to one himself. Perhaps one had to be a shaman, Fargo muttered. It had brought nothing to him. No signs had come his way, no revelations sent through the spirit or the senses. He turned the Ovaro down the slope in the darkness. He rode slowly, no need to hurry now. He'd promised Ellen he'd stop by and he'd keep the promise. But from the direction he rode, Alicia's place was first and he'd stop in for a moment. Alicia would like knowing of his confrontation with Billy Harrison.

He reached the road that lined the base of the hills and turned east as he continued his unhurried way. The moon, almost full now, rose slowly across the black velvet of the sky. He was surprised when he came in sight of the Johnson ranch. Every light in the main house seemed to be on. He rode to a halt, dismounted, and knocked at the door. Alicia pulled the door open in a few moments to stare at him with a frown of surprise, her deep breasts pressed against a cotton work shirt, Levi's tight around her full figure. The surprise was still in her voice when she spoke. "What brings you so early?" she asked.

"Passing by," he said. "Is this a bad time?"

"No, not at all," Alicia said, and his eyes went past her to see the living room in disarray, chairs upended, wall hangings on the floor.

"What happened?" He frowned.

Alicia flung a quick glance back at the room. "I found it like this," she said. "I was away all day visiting Ellie Hodges in Hillsdale. I only got back a few minutes ago." Fargo stepped into the house and saw the door to another room open, books thrown to the floor from shelves, a desk with every drawer emptied out. "The whole house is like that," Alicia said. She walked with him as he stepped into the adjoining room, which was plainly a study. He saw a small wall safe that hung open with papers scattered on the floor in front of it.

"Looks as though you had visitors when you were gone," Fargo commented as he walked into the next room, where more books had been thrown from shelves and scattered around the floor, many left opened.

Another small desk had been emptied, he saw, and two vases lay on their sides on the floor. "They sure were looking for something. I've never seen a place torn apart like this. Got any idea what they were looking for?"

"I suppose money," Alicia said.

"Thieves after money don't take a place apart like this," Fargo said. "They looked inside every book, even took down your wall hangings to look in the back of them. No, they were after something more than money."

Alicia looked wide-eyed at him with a helpless shrug. "What? I certainly don't know," she said, and walked with him into the guest room where he had slept. That, too, had been torn apart, even the mattress cut open. He glanced into the room across the hall, Alicia's bedroom, where she had taken him. It was the only room untouched.

"I think they must've been interrupted before they got to my room," Alicia said. "Todd, my foreman, told me he'd come knocking just after dark to see if I were home. I'd guess they cut out after that."

"None of your hands saw them?" Fargo queried.

"No. I asked," Alicia said. "If they sneaked in the back door, they could've made it without being seen." Fargo turned and walked back through the rooms, Alicia beside him, his eyes sweeping the ransacked rooms again.

"What could they have been after here?" Fargo asked as he paused at the door? "Think, Alicia. That could be the key to everything that's happened. What could Tom have hidden away in the house?"

"I don't know," Alicia said.

"Sleep on it. Think some more. I'll be back tomorrow," Fargo said, more harshly than he'd intended. Alicia nodded, slid her arms around him for a moment, and pressed her breasts tight against him.

"Tomorrow night. I'll be waiting," she said, and he hurried from the house and climbed into the saddle, his lips a thin line. A new dimension had been added. Maybe power, greed, hate, or vengeance hadn't been the reason Tom Johnson had been murdered while he lay helpless on the operating table. Something else had been proven now: whoever planned the killings at Doc Schubert's was still very much on the scene. And so were Royd Haggard, Zach Traynor, and Billy Harrison, Fargo reminded himself. Perhaps examining new reasons might pinpoint one of them, he pondered. It was something he'd have to give new thought to, he realized as he came in sight of Ellen's place.

A dim glow from deep in the house told him she was in one of the back rooms and he waited after his knock until he heard the latch bolt slide back. She opened the door, the big Savage and North in her hand. Her eyes widened with welcome as she saw him and he stepped into the house. But she quickly pulled a glower to her face. "I expected you'd stop by before this," she said, her tone accusing.

"Had to do some things," he said.

"You knew I'd be waiting and worrying," she snapped.

"I knew," he said, and she glared back.

"You see Billy?" she asked.

"I did. He's still alive, if that's what you're wanting to know," Fargo said.

"I want to know if you think he's the one," she answered.

"He could be. I'm not sure about any of them yet," he said. He told her of stopping at the ranch and what he had found there and she frowned as he finished. "Can you think of what your pa might have hidden in the house?"

"No, I can't. His sales receipts and account books, of course. But they were never hidden away. Anybody could find them in his study," Ellen said.

"He keep a key to a secret lockbox at the bank?" Fargo asked.

"Not that I know about. Daddy wasn't one for secret lockboxes. I know he kept his money in the bank at Clay Springs," Ellen said.

"There had to be something. The place was torn apart. Somebody was looking damn hard for something," Fargo said. "Maybe I ought to pay another visit to old Amos."

"You said you were satisfied he'd been honest with you." She frowned.

"I was, until tonight. Now I'm not sure about anything," Fargo muttered. "I'll think on it some more."

"You're still welcome to stay," Ellen said. "I've an extra room."

"I'll take you up on that tonight," Fargo said. "And I'll keep in mind that your invitations have limits."

"You admitting that Alicia's didn't?" she shot back quickly, the question a sideways probe, and he laughed.

"No, I'm just using your words," he said.

"Stable your horse and I'll get the extra room ready," she said, and hurried away. He went outside, took the Ovaro into the stable at the rear of the house, unsaddled the horse, and hung a feed bag in the stall for him. When he returned, he slipped the latch bolt on and Ellen called to him from the back of the house. He found the way to a small but neat room, a single window at the rear, a brass bedstand and a narrow bed along with a lamp and low dresser. "I didn't promise you anything fancy," she said.

"This'll do fine," he said. "Think about what I asked you. What could your pa have hidden in the house?"

"I have been and I can't come up with anything, but I'll keep trying," Ellen said, and paused at the doorway to look back. "This gets more and more complicated, doesn't it? I wonder if maybe it's too much, too big. Maybe it's something we'll never know and we'll have to live with that."

"No, dammit," Fargo snapped. "The damn answer is somewhere in front of me. I can feel it, taste it. I just can't pin it down yet. Maybe this latest thing will help."

"Sleep on it," Ellen said, took a sudden few steps back into the room, and brushed his cheek with her lips. "Thanks for trying so hard," she said, and hurried away.

He heard the door to her room close, down just a few steps from his. He undressed and stretched out on the bed. His reply to Ellen had been all too true, he grimaced and wrestled with frustration. Something was missing. But what? he asked himself again. It danced just out of his reach, tantalizing him. But it was there, as surely as Royd Haggard, Zach Traynor, and Billy Harrison were there. He had to find it, he told himself again as he dropped off to sleep.

He guessed he'd been asleep for two hours or so when he woke, the sound of horses' hooves drifting through the window to him. He sat up, swung from the bed and had trousers on when he heard the knocking at the front door. He waited as he strapped on his gunbelt and stepped to the doorway of the room to see Ellen emerge from her room, sleep still in her face, her robe wrapped around her tall slenderness. But she had the big Savage and North in her hand, he noted, and she saw him in the doorway and her eyes questioned. "Answer it," he whispered, and stayed in the doorway, the Colt in his hand as Ellen went to the door. She unbolted the door and pulled it partly open and he heard a man's voice.

"You Ellen Johnson?" the voice asked, and Ellen nodded.

"Amos Dillon sent us to fetch you," the man said.

"He's been hurt," a second voice put in.

"Hurt?" Ellen echoed, concern in her voice at once. "How?"

"He stumbled carrying his rifle. It went off and shot him," the first voice answered. "We came across him as we were riding through the hills. He asked us to fetch you."

"Wait. I'll get dressed," Ellen said as she closed the door. She hurried back to where Fargo waited, her eyes wide.

"It's possible," he whispered. "Anything's possible. But I don't like it. I don't see a man experienced as Amos having that kind of stupid accident."

"What do I do?" Ellen asked.

"Get dressed, get your horse, and go with them," Fargo said, and Ellen's eyes grew round with surprise and apprehension. "I'll be on your trail." He smiled and her face relaxed. She strode to her room and Fargo threw on the rest of his clothes, opened the window, and slipped from the house. He moved along the rear of the house to the stable, leaving the two men waiting at the front door. He had the Ovaro saddled when Ellen arrived to get her horse. He put a finger to his lips as she saw him and she saddled her mount and climbed onto the horse. She had put on leather, flaring riding culottes and a white blouse, he saw, and she cast him a quick glance as she rode from the stable.

He waited, listened to her ride off with the two men, and then nosed the Ovaro from the saddle. He halted, listened again, and picked up their progress. They were heading down the road and he followed, hung back far enough so he could just hear them moving at a canter. Suddenly the sound of hoofbeats changed tone. They had left the road and were moving along grass-covered slopes into the hills, and he moved forward more quickly.

The nearly full moon let him glimpse the three horses as they went upward, past tree cover, and cut through a rocky section of slope. He swerved, moved to the right of the three horses, and let himself draw closer. He spied a stand of oak and slipped into it and put the pinto into a fast canter that brought him close to Ellen and the two men. He could see them clearly a few dozen feet to his left and below. But the tree cover was thinning fast. Soon he'd be in open land on the rock slopes and he saw Ellen pull her horse back.

"Amos doesn't live in this part of the hills," Fargo heard her say.

"We're takin' a shortcut," one of the men answered, and Fargo saw a thick-necked figure with a fleshy face. But the man slowed his horse as they came to a small rock plateau that dropped off sharply on three sides. With a sudden backward swipe of his arm, the man struck out and Fargo saw Ellen knocked from her horse. She hit the ground, lay there for an instant, and started to rise, but the two men were on her, yanking her to her feet.

"We ain't goin' to just kill her, are we?" the second one whined. "We ought to enjoy her first."

"Just what I aim to do," the thick-necked one said.

"Bastards," Fargo heard Ellen spit out as she tried to twist away, but the second man, taller and thin-faced, grabbed her legs and both threw her onto the flat rock. The thin-faced one was starting to pull her riding culottes off despite Ellen's attempts to kick at him, and he laughed, a high-pitched, whining sound. Fargo drew his Colt, cursed, and put the gun back in its holster. They were too close to Ellen to risk a shot, especially in the moonlight.

"Damn," Fargo swore aloud as he sent the pinto racing out of the trees and down the steep slope. The thin-faced one had Ellen's culottes off and Fargo saw the flash of long, lovely legs as she continued to strike out.

"That's enough, bitch," the man snarled as he smashed the back of his hand across Ellen's face and she cried out in pain. But Fargo was halfway down the short rocky slope now and saw the thick-necked one look up.

"Shit, we got company," the man said, and the other one turned to look up at the horse and rider coming at them. The thick-necked one rose and yanked Ellen to her feet with him, held her in front of him as Fargo reached the flat little plateau. Fargo saw both men draw their guns and he dived from the Ovaro, hit the ground on both feet, and flung himself behind the nearest rock. He rose up enough to peer out and a shot sent rock splinters a few inches from him.

"Let her go," Fargo called out. "Nobody has to get killed."

"Somebody's gonna get killed. You, mister," the

thick-necked one said. " 'Less you come out with your hands up."

"Then, what?"

"We might let you hightail it out of here," the man said, and Fargo grunted derisively. He moved to the other edge of the rock and peered out again. The thick-necked one still held Ellen in front of him as an effective shield. The taller one was close beside him, but both were edging toward their horses. Ellen, the man's arm around her neck and pressing hard, was helpless, Fargo saw. His eyes went to the thin, taller one again. The man was staying close to Ellen but not close enough, Fargo decided. He'd reduce the odds by 50 percent, and he raised the Colt, took aim, and fired. The thin form flew backward as though he'd been kicked by a mule, slammed into the side of a rock, and slid to the ground, leaving a swatch of red along the rock.

Fargo saw the thick-necked man put his gun to Ellen's ribs. "You shoot again and she gets it," the man threatened.

"Let her go. I just want some answers," Fargo said.

"Go to hell," the man threw back as he reached his horse.

"I'm coming after you. You'll never outride me carrying her along. Let her go," Fargo said. The man didn't answer for a moment and then he backed a few paces and Fargo saw him halt at the edge of the plateau where it fell off in a sharp drop.

"Throw your gun out or she goes over the side," the man said. Fargo swore softly and realized he had no choice. He sent the Colt slithering across the rock flooring as the man moved back to his horse. "Now come out," the man ordered.

"And be gunned down? No, thanks," Fargo said.

"Out, dammit," the man snarled.

"No," Fargo said. His refusal played with Ellen's life, he realized, but if he let the man gun him down, she was as good as dead. He was banking on the man's decision to keep her as his hole card. He waited and watched the man move his horse back a few steps. With a sudden whirling motion, the man leapt onto the horse and sent Ellen flying over the edge of the plateau all in one motion and Fargo's curse was drowned out by Ellen's scream.

The man was racing off on his horse as Fargo ran from behind the rock. With the survival of the cunning, the man had left him with a devil's choice, and he counted on the decision that was made as Fargo ran to the edge of the plateau. Ellen lay some two dozen feet below, but the falloff had not been entirely sheer, he saw. She had bounced and rolled down a rocky slope to where she lay unmoving. He raced back to the Ovaro, took his lariat, wrapped one end around a slab of rock, and lowered himself over the side.

Reaching the bottom of the drop, he knelt beside Ellen and found with relief that she was alive though unconscious. He carefully moved her arms and legs, and all her appendages seemed to respond properly. There were no broken bones, he was satisfied, but her body had taken a bruising tumble. He lifted her, coiled the lariat around her waist as well as his, and began to pull himself up the side of the rock wall. He had gone halfway when his back and shoulder muscles began to cramp with the strain. He paused, resting both feet against the stone side of the drop. He rested for almost a full minute to let his muscles loosen. When he started to pull himself upward again, one arm around Ellen's unconscious form, he let his back arch backward to counter some of the muscle strain. The last dozen feet of the climb found his arms and shoulders burning with pain and he used his legs to press against the stone wall. Yet each pull with the deadweight of Ellen's unconscious form had become a teeth-gritting moment of agony.

He knew it had been only minutes, but it seemed hours before he reached the ledge and pulled himself and Ellen over the top. He lay prone, drawing in deep gulps of air until his normal breathing returned. He pushed to his feet.

Ellen moaned as he took the lariat from around her and he saw her eyes flicker as he lifted her onto the Ovaro with him. Her mount followed the Ovaro as Fargo slowly started back down the slope. Ellen moaned again and this time her eyes pulled open. She craned her neck to look back at him. "Oh, God, I thought I was dead," she murmured.

"You were lucky," he said.

"I hurt all over," she muttered.

"Don't talk now," he said, and she leaned back against him in silence as he rode through the dark. He kept the horse at a walk to avoid jouncing her unnecessarily and finally reached her place with the moon curving down the far reaches of the sky. He swung to the ground, lifted her from the saddle, and carried her to the house.

"My room," she said, and he took her into a smallish bedroom with ruffled curtains, a tall dresser, and a wide bed with cotton sheets still turned down. She winced as he set her on the bed.

"Where's that salve you used on me?" he asked.

"Top of the dresser. Brown jar," Ellen said. He rose and found the jar. She was on her side when he returned to the bed. "I'll put it on," she said.

"You can't reach your back," Fargo said firmly. "Turn over."

Ellen gasped in pain but obeyed and rolled onto her stomach. He sat down at the edge of the bed, pulled up her shirt, and looked at a smooth, strong back, slender and curving into a small waist. It was lovely despite the red bruise marks. "You were right. It was all a trick," Ellen said as he opened the jar of salve.

"They had orders to take you someplace and get rid of you," Fargo said.

"Why?"

"Maybe they expect I'll back off if you're killed." Fargo frowned.

"That'd still leave Alicia to keep you on," Ellen said, and Fargo felt her words strike at him as though they were a physical blow.

"Alicia," he echoed. "Jesus, Alicia. Maybe they went after her, too." He thrust the jar at Ellen as he leapt to his feet, his lips drawn back in a grimace. "You rest. I'll be back as soon as I can," he said as he raced from the house. He vaulted into the saddle and had the pinto into a full gallop in seconds. He bent low in the saddle as he raced through the last hours of the night, cut across a low hill and down the opposite slope until he came into sight of the big ranch, the buildings sprawled in silent darkness.

He skidded to a halt and was pounding on the door in seconds. Impatiently, he peered into the window when he saw the lamplight go on in the interior of the house and he returned to the door as it opened and Alicia looked at him, kerosene lamp in one hand, the pink nightgown barely encasing her full figure. "You're all right, thank God," he breathed as Alicia frowned at him.

"Yes, I'm fine. Why? What is it?" Alicia frowned.

"They tried to kill Ellen," Fargo said, and Alicia's eyes widened. He threw words at her in terse sentences as he told her what had happened.

"My God," she breathed when he finished. "But she's all right, you say?"

"Yes. Bruised a little but she's all right," Fargo said.

"She's lucky you were there," Alicia said, and he shrugged agreement. Her arms rose, slid around his neck, and her lips pressed his with soft moistness. "That's for rushing to see about me," she murmured. "I don't suppose you'll stay."

"No, I want to go back to her. She's still pretty shaken," Fargo said.

"Of course," Alicia said. "There's always tomorrow night." She drew her arms back and his quick glance took in the room behind her where he saw the wall hangings had been put back in place and the bureau drawers returned to order.

"You've straightened up the house," he said.

"Only the living room. I'll do the rest tomorrow," she said, and walked outside with him.

"Don't go with anyone who shows up, no matter what message they bring, even if they tell you I sent them, understand?" he told her, and she nodded.

"What if it's true? What if you need me?" Alicia asked.

"That'll be too bad for me. You don't go with anybody," he reiterated sternly.

"Yes, sir." Alicia smiled. "Come back soon as you can."

He waved as he rode away and saw her go back into the house. He rode back more slowly than he had come, and when he reached Ellen's, he was pleasantly surprised to find she had struggled up to latch the door. He knocked and it took a few minutes before he heard her on the other side of the door.

"It's me," he called, and listened to the bolt slide back. He pushed the door open and met her eyes round with questions, one hand holding the neck of her robe closed. "Alicia's all right," he said.

"That's good," she said as he closed the door and followed as she shuffled into her room, where she sank down on the bed, still obviously in pain.

"Lie down. I'll finish with the salve," he said, and Ellen turned onto her stomach. He sat down on the edge of the bed, slid the robe from her shoulders, and pulled it down to her waist. He took a moment to admire the broad but nicely rounded shoulders before beginning to apply the salve. His strong fingers could summon sensitivity and he gently smoothed the salve over the bruises on her back. Ellen made little noises, some of pain, but some of pleasure. His hands moved down to the small of her back, massaged gently and the robe slid farther down to show the lovely swell of her rear. He continued to gently massage as his hands came down across the soft rise of her flesh.

"No," she said, a command whispered, almost gasped. "Not now," she added in the same breathy whisper.

"No, not now," he echoed. "Healing time is what you need now. But that almost sounded like a promise."

"Not now," she repeated, her voice muffled as she buried her face in the sheets. He rubbed her back gently again and then rose and put the cap back on the jar.

He left the robe just covering her rear and legs as she lay with her face turned now, one cheek against the sheets, her eyes closed. He glimpsed the flattened swell of the side of one breast as he left her and walked to the extra room where he had slept. The sun was just beginning to edge the top of the distant hills as he undressed and stretched out on the bed. He was too tired to sort out everything that had happened this night. He'd have to find a place for it, but that could wait. He let sleep come to him.

When he woke, the sun was near the noon sky. He rose, used a pitcher of water in a corner of the room to wash, and finally pulled on trousers and gun belt and stepped into the small corridor between the two rooms. The door to Ellen's room was still open, and he paused to look in. She was on the edge of the bed, still in the robe but her face was scrubbed and her hair combed. Her light-blue eyes held his as he stepped into the room, her face serious, almost somber. "You look fine. How do you feel?" he asked.

"Much better. All right, really. That's a miracle salve," Ellen said. Her thin black eyebows took on a faint arch as she leaned back on her elbows and her eyes stayed on him. "I keep thinking about last night and everything you did," she said.

"I'm glad I was here to do it," Fargo said.

"It was wonderful, all of it, but in a funny sort of way one thing stands out. I don't know why," Ellen said thoughtfully. "Your hands rubbing my back. Crazy, isn't it?"

"That ended the night. Last things stay with you," Fargo said.

She gave a half-smile, almost rueful. "That's too logical an explanation," she said as she rose to her feet.

"You've a better one?" he asked.

"Yes," Ellen said, and then her lips were against his cheek, a soft, brushed kiss. But she didn't step back this time. Instead, her lips found his and he felt the warm softness of her kiss, the edge of her tongue touching his mouth for a fleeting instant. He responded, pressed his mouth harder against hers, let his tongue dart in a quick probe, and heard her gasp. He felt her hands move and then the robe come open and warm skin touched his chest, twin points of soft, sensual pressure.

He sank down atop the bed with her. She moved her shoulders and the robe fell away from her. She wore nothing underneath and he let his gaze move across longish breasts that became full-cupped, each topped with a bright-pink nipple on a faint pink areola, a lovely curve to each. Below, he saw a lean rib cage that curved into a flat abdomen and flat belly and, beneath, a very thick and curly black V, the raggedy bushiness thrust upward by the swell of the pubic mound beneath. Long, lean legs followed, thighs thin but not without shape, long calves that were slender yet strong.

He brought his mouth to hers again, pressed, and her lips came open. She answered his probing tongue with her own and he felt her body half-twist as a tiny quiver ran through her. His hand moved slowly across one breast, traced a warm path along the edge, and cupped its fullness. His thumb gently moved back and forth across the bright-pink nipple. "Oh, oh, yes . . . oh, yes," Ellen breathed, and her hands were stroking his shoulder blades. She gasped out again as he brought his mouth to her breast, first one, then the other, pulled gently, drew the full cup up against his tongue. He sucked gently and Ellen cried out, louder this time, a half-laugh, half-gasp. He felt her hand close around the back of his neck to hold his mouth to her breast. His lips closed around the nipple and he felt it quiver, grow firmer in his mouth. Ellen moaned softly.

He kept her breast in his mouth as his hand slid slowly down across her abdomen, paused to circle the tiny indentation in the center of her belly, and moved down farther to push into the dense black V. He let his fingers move idly through the thickness of her nap, felt the rise of her pubic mound, and pressed gently down on it. Ellen moaned again, louder this time as his hand moved back and forth through her denseness. His fingers slid down to the tip of the triangle where her thighs pressed tight together.

His hand moved to the soft smooth skin of one thigh and he felt the dampness of her as Ellen moaned again. He pressed harder against her inner thigh, warm flesh, damp, smooth. His flattened palm slid down between her legs. "Oh, oooooh," Ellen moaned, and her thighs parted, just enough for him to cup his hand around the dark portal. Ellen's moan became a soft cry as he touched the liquescent lips and she drew her knees up, her legs opening, the invitation of invitations. His fingers touched deeper, smoothness, caresses, soft explorings of the senses as her pelvis thrust uwpard, the body answering.

Ellen's hands rubbed against his chest, pressed, pushed harder, and she began to cry out small wailing sounds as he stroked the inner passage of pleasure. Her small wailing sounds increased in pitch as he caressed deeper, increased still more when he drew back to massage the very tip of the now-wet lips. Ellen's hands clasped around his neck and drew his mouth to hers as her hips began to twist and turn. They made upward little thrusting motions and then drew back only to come forward again. Her light-blue eyes had grown not so much lighter, he saw, but had taken on a pale-blue glow, the reflection of an inner flame. "Oh, God, Fargo . . . oh, God," she managed to gasp out between wails. Suddenly her body was heaving and twisting and her arms pulling at him. "Please, please, don't stop . . . make me, take me, make me . . . oh, God," Ellen half-screamed, a torrent of words carried by ecstasy almost beyond enduring.

He came to her, sliding in smoothly along the warm, wet passage, and felt her lean thighs rubbing against his buttocks, lifting, pressing into his sides as she pushed with him. Now her neck arched backward, small blue veins standing out as her head twisted even farther back. The pleasure of all senses risen to new heights, the body immersed in itself, her ecstasy made his and his made hers. Ellen's voice rose in a wailing scream as her climax exploded and her thighs tightened against him. He felt the sweet contractions of her and she was clinging to him with every part of her body, arms, legs, torso hard against him, breasts flattened into his chest. Her scream hung in midair until it finally trailed away into a half-sob of disappointment and her body grew limp.

She fell back, her arms dropping from around his neck. He lay half over her as her lovely breasts rose and fell with each deep breath she drew in. Her eyes found his, almost stared at him as she reached one arm up and drew his face down to hers. "It was wonderful," she breathed as her lips pressed his. "And I never meant for it to happen."

"Maybe it's better that way," he said as he slid his body down to lie beside her. She turned onto her side, breasts dipping, nipples lightly touching his chest.

"I want to just stay here and forget everything else," Ellen murmured.

"Could you?" he asked.

"No," she breathed, sadness in her voice as she rose onto her elbows and pressed down against him, her mouth finding his. "For when it's over," she said, let the kiss linger until she pushed away and rose from him, quick, graceful motions, her body beautifully lean, hips and breasts swinging in unison. He had to fight down the impulse to pull her back to him.

But the questions were already flooding over him, cavorting through his mind, taunting, mocking. He swung from the bed and began to dress.

8

He stayed in the shade of the line of black oak as he slowly rode across the low hills in the afternoon sun. Ellen had left him at the door, the robe pulled loosely around herself, her lips lingering again on his. "What will you do now?" she had asked.

"Try to sort it out. Try to fit in the things that don't fit," he had told her. The reply had been too simple. The things that refused to fit were elusive, dancing inside him as they refused definition. Yet they were there, very much there, intuitive, unformed, and beyond ignoring, a contradiction of the senses. But two elements defied explaining. Why had someone wanted Ellen dead, out of the way? It didn't make sense. Alicia was Tom Johnson's widow. She was the one that would carry on the power and wealth of the Johnson ranch.

Another question crowded the first. What had they searched for so desperately at Alicia's? He could come up with no answer for that, but he was certain of one thing: whoever had Alicia's house torn apart had also ordered Ellen killed. There was a connection someplace. But what? He swore softly as he pushed aside the question that refused answering. That answer would fall in place only when he could pinpoint whoever planned the killings at Doc Schubert's.

He pulled the pinto to a halt in the shade of a big red ash, slid to the ground, and sat down against the dark-gray, fissured bark. He put his head back, relaxed his body, and let thoughts flow freely, determined to reexamine every detail of what he had learned.

He'd begin with Royd Haggard and sift through all he knew until the picture was complete. Royd Haggard had motive, one of the oldest of motives, envy and greed. He also had the money to buy hired killers. He was in the right place to put it all together. And he was the smartest of the three, a man who had built a successful cattle ranch, a man who knew how to plan and how to execute his plans. He also had the most to gain by killing Tom Johnson. Ambition and power always went beyond mere personal satisfaction. Royd Haggard had to stay at the head of the list, Fargo decided.

And yet, Fargo grimaced, something still refused to fit. Little thoughts continued to nag and something else he still couldn't define continued to dance just out of reach. Finally, he put Royd Haggard aside and turned his thoughts to Zach Traynor. He carefully took Zach Traynor apart in his thoughts. The man's motive was simple hate. By firing him, Tom Johnson had not only marked him as a thief but had reduced his life to that of a low-paid ranch hand. Zach Traynor was sullen, cunning, and cowardly, and the killings at Doc Schubert's had been cunning and cowardly, a man murdered as he lay helpless on an operating table. It was the kind of killing Zach Traynor could plan. It fitted his weasel's character.

But there were things about Zach Traynor that didn't fit, and Fargo spat in disgust as he let his thoughts turn to Billy Harrison. The youth had perhaps the oldest and most powerful motive of all, more powerful than greed or power or simple hate. Billy Harrison held revenge inside him, revenge, the emotion that consumes mind and body. He was also arrogant enough to have enjoyed planning Tom Johnson's murder. There was another fact that stood out. After his affair with Ellen had been destroyed, Billy Harrison had no reason to stay around Clay Springs except for a chance for vengeance. Zach Traynor stayed because he needed a job to pay for his drinking and gambling. Royd Haggard had to stay because his roots were here. But Billy Harrison could have taken off for anyplace. Yet he had stayed close. It was a fact that couldn't be ignored.

But Fargo found his lips drawing back again. As with the others, things about Billy Harrison didn't quite fit right. Yet that wasn't enough. Something else gnawed at him. It had done so from the very beginning. He hadn't been able to give it shape or form, but it had been there, adding to his inability to zero in on Royd Haggard, Traynor, or Billy Harrison. Something little, lurking in the mind, refusing to come forward. Some thoughts were like wild mustangs, he decided. They fought at being harnessed, refused to come when summoned. You had to let them come to you on their own.

He half-smiled as he shook away further musings, suddenly aware that the day had disappeared behind the hills. He rose and climbed into the saddle as the darkness swept the land, and he rode down the slope and turned east. When he halted, he was on a hillock that let him see Ellen's place. He waited till he glimpsed her through the windows before he turned away. His next stop was in the trees near the Johnson ranch, where again he waited until he saw Alicia moving about inside the house. He turned away, finally, and rode on. Both Ellen and Alicia were safe inside. Both knew to be careful. This was not a night for stopping to talk or to make love. This was a night to think again, to search the mind again. This was a night to let the wild-mustang thoughts come of their own free will.

He rode back to the red ash, but this time he stretched out on his bedroll and let his mind travel backward, to that moment when he had approached Doc Schubert's office. He closed his eyes as he reached back to relive every moment since that fateful dusk. But no pulling on thoughts now. He'd let the mind run free as, step by step, he relived every single minute. It would be quite like walking back over a trail to see if a footprint had been missed, a sign overlooked, a mark undetected. But this trail would take him through the forest of the mind. He lay back and closed his eyes and let the past become real again.

His mind became a conductor and he felt himself slip into a kind of half-sleep that stretched time into nothingness and made the world into an inner place. The moon had drifted far across the night sky when Fargo's eyes suddenly snapped open; he sat up. He felt the frown digging into his brow as he stared into space, seeing nothing for a long moment. Thoughts stopped tumbling through his mind. Instead, they lined up in orderly formation and everything that had refused to fit suddenly made sense. He wanted to laugh, to feel exultation, but he could only feel a sense of awe. He had his answer. It had been there all the time, lurking, hidden away, yet there in the back of his mind.

He had his answer and yet he knew he had to carry it to that final confirmation, that moment when certainty became proof. Conviction was not enough. He wanted admission. And there were still a few questions unanswered. But he had enough for now. He lay back, suddenly feeling drained. He let sleep close his eyes as a grim satisfaction curled inside him. There'd be justice for Doc Schubert and the others: a small gift but the only one he had to give.

He slept till the sun had fully cleared the top of the hills, and when he rose, he washed at a pond and breakfasted at a stand of wild cherry. He took his time. There was no need for hurrying now. He watched a flock of indigo buntings cavort in the warm air, their dusty-blue color heightened in the morning sun, as he made plans for what he had to do. Simple plans, a variation this time, another kind of bait. He let the day slide into the afternoon before he slowly rode from the hills and made his way to the Clay Springs Playhouse.

There were more than enough regulars inside the saloon for his purposes. What he had to say would be on its way within minutes after he left the bar, he was certain. His sweeping glance paused to see Goldie was already at her usual place at the end of the bar and he nodded to her as he stepped forward. "Was wondering what happened to you, friend," the bartender said. "You haven't stopped by lately."

"Been busy," Fargo said.

"You're early today," the bartender commented.

"The early bird gets the worm," Fargo said, and the man's brows edged upward slightly. Fargo chose his words and let them slide from his lips in a firm, clear voice. "Last time I was here only one person knew who had Tom Johnson killed. Now there are two of us who know," he said, and the bartender's eyebrows went higher. Fargo heard the silence come over the others. "I'll be waiting at the foot of Ridge Hill at dawn. He knows who he is. This'll be his last chance to come after me before I hunt him down."

"Guess that makes it final enough," the bartender said.

"Very final," Fargo agree. "A guilty man gets a last chance, he'll show for it." He turned and strode to where Goldie sat, her tight blond curls unchanged by even a stray hair. "Billy Harrison's not a man to live without a woman. One of your girls has been visiting him," Fargo said.

"Maybe," the woman allowed.

"Send her to him. Tell her to tell him what I said."

"What if he's not the one?" the woman asked.

"Then he won't show up," Fargo answered. She nodded and he turned and strode from the bar. His lips wore a thin smile as he rode slowly from town. The last challenge had been flung out. He had no reservations about who would show up, but he needed that final proof. He made his way to Ellen's as dusk settled over the land, and he saw her face at the window as he swung from the saddle. She had the bolt unlatched in seconds and ran to him, breasts bouncing under a green cotton shirt.

"Where've you been?" she asked. "I've been so worried about you."

"Sorting things out. I know who killed your father," he told her. Ellen's lips fell open as she stared at him.

"Who?" she bit out. "Who was it?"

"I'll have the final proof, come dawn. I'll tell you when it's done," he said.

"You can tell me now. You said you knew."

"There's knowing and there's proving. I want it nailed down."

"How will you know, come dawn?" Ellen asked,

and he told her what he had done at the bar and saw protest flood her face. "You can't, not that way. You're asking to be killed," she said.

"I don't plan to let that happen," he said.

"What if all three of them show up?"

"They won't. There's no need for that. The only one with any reason to show is the guilty one."

"Tell me," Ellen said. "I've a right to know. What if something happens to you?"

"Then you'll be safer not knowing," Fargo said.

Ellen's arms slid around his neck and her mouth was on his. "Don't do this, not this way," she said. "I'm afraid. Maybe you don't need that proof."

"It's nothing without that, honey," he said, and stepped back. "I'll be going now. I want to leave myself plenty of time."

She swallowed hard, fought back tears that welled up in her eyes. "You tell Alicia what you told me?" she asked.

"Not yet," he said. "I intend to."

"Maybe she can convince you not to do this," Ellen said with an edge of waspishness suddenly flaring.

He smiled. "Alicia has a bigger stake than you in this," he said.

"He was my father," Ellen bit out.

"So he was, but that doesn't change what I said," he returned. "Lock your door. I'll come back as soon as it's over." He pulled the door closed and heard her slam the bolt shut as he rode away.

The night had grown deep when he reached the Johnson ranch, the bunkhouse dark and still. Alicia opened the door at his knock, a silk dressing gown encasing her full figure, and her arms encircled him at once.

"God, you know how to make a person wonder and worry," she said.

"Sorry about that," he said. "But I know who killed Tom," he said, and Alicia's full face grew fuller with a rush of surprise. He quickly told her much the same thing he had told Ellen, and she continued to frown at him when he finished. "That's a hard way to get proof," she said.

"It's the best way. Confession with a Colt," he said.

"Who is it? I deserve to know," Alicia said.

"I'll give you a chance to find out same time I do," Fargo said. "Get dressed. I'll need your help."

She stared for another moment at him. "Whatever you want," Alicia said, and hurried away as he waited by the door. She returned dressed in a dark-green shirt and leather riding culottes. "I'll get my horse," she said, and he waited beside the Ovaro. He tightened the cinch strap and made a few other adjustments and was in the saddle when she returned on a brown mare. She had strapped on a gun belt, he saw, with a Wells-Fargo Colt in the holster.

"You won't need that," he said. "I've something better for you."

"What am I going to do in this?" Alicia asked.

"I'll tell you when we get there," he said, and she fell silent as he led the way along the base of the hills. There was less than a half-hour to dawn when he reached the foot of Ridge Hill and he found a tall box elder that grew out from the other trees. He rode past it into the tree cover that formed a backdrop to it, slid from the saddle, and took a moment to scan the terrain in front of him as the first gray light began to tint the land. Satisfied, he turned to Alicia, who had swung to the ground, and he led her horse and the Ovaro deeper into the trees.

When he turned, he took the rifle from the saddle holster and handed it to her. "You're going to take this and stay back of the tree. I'll be in front and I can see every approach to it, but nothing is sure. There's a good amount of high brush and rock. If the killer manages to get the drop on me, you'll be there as backup," he said.

"Yes," Alicia said. "You've no worries." She came forward, her eyes searching his. "Thanks for bringing me," she said.

"It's only right." He smiled and she stepped back as he started to walk away to take his position in front of the big box elder.

"I'm still betting on Royd Haggard," she said, and he smiled as he leaned back against the gray-brown bark, the Colt in his hand. His gaze swept the land at the foot of the rise that led to the hill, lingered on the patches of high brush, and moved on. Daybreak had begun to slowly roll down from the top of the hills, the dawn hour on the land. But nothing moved in front of him. The dawn grew lighter as the minutes went by and still nothing moved. He flicked his glance to the two lines of trees that climbed along the sides of the hills. Only the flight of morning birds broke the stillness there.

Fargo's face remained impassive, but he let his lips purse. The dawn continued to lighten. The sun was moving close to peering over the tops of the hills at his back, he realized. He'd expected his final proof for at least the last fifteen minutes, and the thought raced through him: had he been wrong? It clung for a brief moment before he shook it away. He was in a half-crouch against the tree when the shot came, from slightly to the left and behind him. He pitched forward, his legs collapsing under him, and he lay half on his side, one arm outstretched when he came to a halt.

The second shot came as he lay there, the sound of the big Sharps unmistakable. He lay still, his eyes hardly more than slits, his lips drawn back in a grimace. The footsteps approached, halted, and Fargo glimpsed the end of the rifle barrel. His arm exploded in an uwpard arc, fingers closing around the rifle as he did so. He yanked and leapt to his feet and saw Alicia fall sideways as he pulled the gun from her grasp. She landed on one knee, her eyes wide as she looked up at him.

"I took the bullets out before I gave it to you," he said, waving the big Sharps. Alicia rose and her eyes were narrowed as she stared at him. "You arranged the killings at Doc Shubert's, Alicia," he said. "You planned it and hired the killers."

Alicia's eyes stayed narrowed. "How did you know?" she asked.

"It took me a while. You were clever, real clever."

"Why look to me? You had Royd Haggard. He fitted in every way."

"Almost. I had to look real hard at him," Fargo admitted. "But he was too smart a man for it."

"Too smart?"

"That's right. Everyone knew he had threatened Tom. And everyone knew he had the most to gain by Tom's death. He was too smart a man to plan something that would make him the chief suspect," Fargo said.

"He sent men to kill you. Didn't that prove it?"

"They had orders to beat me up. The killing part got out of hand. It was a stupid move on his part, but it didn't change the rest," Fargo said.

"Zach Traynor?" Alicia asked.

"If Royd Haggard was too smart to do it, Traynor was too stupid. This took someone clever, and hired killers cost money. Zach Traynor didn't have enough money to fix his boots or buy a new gun belt much less to pay hired guns," Fargo said. "He didn't have the brains or the money to do it."

He watched Alicia's full lips purse as she turned his answer in her mind. "Billy Harrison," she said.

"Billy Harrison fancies himself a gunfighter. He tried to face me down. He would've done the same with Tom Johnson. He wouldn't have hired killers. He had reasons and opportunity, but it was out of character for him," Fargo answered. "They all had reasons. They all fitted. And none of them fitted right."

"What turned you onto me?" Alicia asked, and he smiled.

"Little things. Always look for the little things," Fargo said. "I couldn't catch hold of them for a while. Then you fell into place and the rest followed."

"Such as?"

"I told you and Ellen to keep your doors latched. Ellen always had her latch bolt on and she answered the door with a gun in hand. But you never had your latch on, not once. That stuck in the back of my mind until I suddenly realized why. You knew nobody was going to come after you," Fargo said. "Then all the other things that had been stuck deep inside me began to surface."

"Tell me. I'm curious," Alicia said.

"You gave such unusually good descriptions of the three killers. Three men burst in while your husband is being operated on and kill everybody. You were diving for cover to avoid being killed, yet you supplied

149

a perfect description of them. You even noted the scar on the lip of one of them. And in all that excitement, you managed to hear them say where they were going.'' Fargo smiled. ''Having them shoot you in the leg was a nice touch. Sending me after them was a brilliant stroke. I'd kill them and there'd be nobody left who knew the truth except you. You'd have been home free if I hadn't seen that it really wasn't a random robbery.''

Alicia's voice took on an edge. ''You were an unexpected interruption and I didn't expect you'd be so sharp.''

''You didn't stop being clever. You sent me looking for a trail in the Smokey Hills. That gave you three days to find Amos Dillon and have him killed just in case he knew anything that could backfire on you,'' Fargo said, and admitted a note of admiration into his voice. ''All of it stuck deep inside me. I couldn't bring it out. Maybe I never would have if you'd latched your door the way Ellen did. Little things, honey. Always the little things.''

Alicia's smile was fashioned of venom. ''I'll remember that,'' she said.

''Tell me one thing I haven't been able to put in place,'' Fargo said. ''You were the one who tore your house apart. That story you gave me was a piece of fast thinking. What were you looking for?''

''Tom's will. He told me he had left everything to Ellen. Everything, the old bastard. That's when I decided to have him killed. I figured I'd just tear up the will afterward,'' Alicia said.

''Only you couldn't find it,'' Fargo said, and she nodded.

''Not anywhere. It wasn't in the safe where it should've been. It wasn't anywhere. That's when I realized he'd hidden it someplace and I took the place apart to find it.''

"Did you?" Fargo queried.

"No, dammit," Alicia snapped.

"That's when you decided you had to get rid of Ellen," he said, and she shot him a baleful glare. "Take that gun you have and drop it on the ground," Fargo said, drawing his own Colt. "Very carefully now."

Alicia obeyed, drawing the revolver from its holster with two fingers and letting it drop on the ground. The shot exploded the moment the gun hit the ground. No empty rifle this time and he felt the pain as the bullet grazed the side of his head. The pain became instant burning and the dizziness swept through him. He knew he was falling forward and he could do nothing about it. He hit the ground still half-conscious and lay there as the pain continued to sweep through him. He shook his head, tried to fight off the wave of darkness that threatened to engulf him, but the pain made him gasp. The dark curtain descended, the world vanished.

Voices. Dim sounds in his mind. He pulled his eyes open and saw only a blur. The voices grew stronger and he shook his head and groaned at the stab of pain. But the blur began to dissolve. It hadn't been long, he realized out of some conscious understanding, and he moved his arms. They responded and he fought away the pain as he shook his head again and the blue vanished completely. He looked up and saw Alicia, a man beside her. The thick-necked one with the fleshy face that had gotten away after seizing Ellen.

"This is Burt," Alicia said. "After you saved Ellen's neck, I got a little edgy. I didn't think you'd ever come onto me, but I wanted some insurance. I gave Burt orders to stay in the trees, and if he saw me leave the house, he was to follow me, no matter who I was with or where I went. Standing orders.''

"So when he saw you ride off with me tonight, he just followed," Fargo said grimly as he pushed to his feet.

"The little things, remember?" Alicia said, and laughed as he cursed silently. She had her gun back in her holster and his Colt stuck in her belt.

"You intend to get rid of me now," Fargo said.

"Very much so. But not here and not by bullets. I don't want little Ellen or anybody else asking questions. No more poking around from anybody," Alicia said. "We're going high up into the hills where you're going to have a terrible fall and smash your head."

"Only I'll do the smashing," the man snarled.

"Get on your horse," Alicia ordered, and pushed the rifle back into its saddle holster. She swung in behind him, the revolver in hand and pointed at his back. The man moved out a few paces in front of him. Fargo swore silently again as Burt rode up a steep passage that grew less steep but continued to climb. He saw the land grow heavier with tree cover and dotted with sharp-edged rock formations. The man made his way through a passage barely wide enough for the horses to move single-file. Rock and thick tree cover rose up on each side. Peering past the man, Fargo saw the land level a little but the trees and rocks remained heavy.

"This looks good," the man called back as the land leveled further. Fargo saw the sharp drop-off of rock at one side, the thick stand of black oak on the other. He was running out of time. He cast a glance behind him at Alicia. She had the revolver trained directly at him and he swore silently. He'd never be able to reach the throwing knife in its calf holster around his leg. The small, almost flat patch of land appeared, and the man halted, swung from his horse, and Fargo reined the Ovaro to a stop.

"Get off," Alicia ordered, and Fargo swung to the ground. The heavy tree cover was not more than a foot away, he saw and grimaced inwardly. Alicia's gun was not much farther away. "Use the stock of his rifle, Burt," she said, and Fargo watched the man pull the Sharps from its saddle case. Alicia stayed in the saddle as she moved her horse so that she faced Fargo. "Put your hands behind your back," she ordered, and Fargo obeyed. He saw Burt move behind him and start to raise the rifle by its barrel. Their plan was simple, he realized. Smash his head in and then throw him over the sharp drop-off. It would look thoroughly convincing when he was found, his head smashed in by the fall.

He tensed his every muscle. He would have perhaps two or three seconds to remain alive. Alicia would give him that, unable not to. She didn't want him found shot. She'd hold back firing, an automatic reaction. He held his breath, let the senses quiver undisturbed. He felt the movement of air strike the back of his neck as the man swung the rifle, held for another split second, and then dropped. The rifle stock scraped the top of his head as he went down and dived forward. He heard Alicia's combined curse and scream, but she still hadn't fired as he crashed into the trees.

"Don't let him get away," Alicia screamed, and Fargo rolled into the thick brush, his hand yanking the double-edged blade from its calf holster. He saw Burt, six-gun in hand, start to rush into the trees, and Alicia, staying on her horse, peered after him, her gun raised. The trees were thick, but only a small cluster with little room to move. The man would find him in seconds.

Fargo raised the perfectly balanced knife, gripped it in his palm as he crouched low. Burt advanced toward him, his pistol raised, his eyes sweeping the brush. Suddenly the man halted, found his quarry, and Fargo had to strike with no more time to aim. He flung the knife with an upward motion and the blade hurtled out of the brush just as Burt fired. Fargo pulled his head sideways and felt the heat of the bullet that whizzed past him. He saw the blade strike, but the throw had been hurried. The knife struck into the man's shoulder and Burt's second shot went wild.

He tried to bring his gun around with the knife blade still in his shoulder, but Fargo was charging out of the brush. He slammed into the man as the pistol fired again, another shot that went wild. Burt went over onto his back and Fargo's fingers closed over his gun hand. Fargo drove his forearm into the man's throat and heard the gargling, choking sound that followed. Burt's grip on the gun relaxed and Fargo twisted the weapon from his hand, but the two shots exploded before he could get his own grip on the gun. Alicia fired again and he had to fling himself into a roll as the gun skidded into the brush.

He came to a halt and peered to see that Alicia was still in the saddle, at the edge of the trees, still peering into the thick leaves. Burt, coughing and wheezing, struggled up onto one knee, breathing harshly through his injured trachea. He reached one hand across himself and tore the knife from his shoulder, flung it on the ground as he tried to push to his feet. The blade was less than a dozen feet away, Fargo saw from the brush where he lay. But he'd never reach it with Alicia peering in, poised to shoot. Burt, still gasping and wheezing, continued to pour through the brush to find his gun.

Fargo cursed silently. There was no time for calm decisions. He reached out, vigorously shook a bush while he rolled to his left at the same time.

Alicia fired, three shots, and Fargo smiled as he leapt to his feet and tore from the brush. Alicia was attempting to reload, saw him come into sight, and flung her gun aside. But he had reached the knife as she was still pulling Fargo's Colt from wherever she'd tucked it into her waist. Burt half-spun, still gagging, breath coming with difficulty. But he had found his gun and he started to complete his turn when Fargo flung the blade, a proper, overhand throw this time. Burt's breathing grew more difficult as the blade hurtled into the base of his throat, the hilt the only part of it still visible as he toppled backward.

Fargo dived to his left. Alicia would have the Colt out by now, he knew, and her shot slammed into the brush where he had been. She had given up the plan for a fake accident. Killing him was more important. Fargo dropped low as another shot hurtled into the trees. He leapt up, raced back the other way in the small, confined area, and Alicia's third shot went wild. Alicia was good at many things but marksmanship was not one of them, he saw. She recognized that, also as he saw her yank the horse around and start to race off. She was going to give herself more distance, make him come out of the trees onto the openness of the small plateau where she could take better aim.

Fargo raced from the trees into the open, his powerful legs driving him forward after the horse. Alicia turned in the saddle to see him streaking after her, and she fired, a hasty, wild shot that passed harmless to his left. He swerved to the right as he saw her bringing the gun around to fire again and the shot passed wide of him again. "One more, honey," he muttered aloud as he continued to face forward.

Alicia yanked her horse to a halt as she realized she needed to be stationary to fire with any degree of accuracy. Fargo saw her bring the Colt around, but hold fire, determined not to miss in haste this time. He swerved to his right, saw her follow with the Colt. She did the same as he swerved left, still racing toward her. His lips were pulled back as he dived straight forward, the move taking her by surprise. She fired, but surprise had lost her those precious split seconds, and he felt the bullet graze the back of his legs as he hit the ground.

He leapt to his feet as Alicia pulled the trigger again and heard only the click of the hammer on an empty chamber. She waited, the Colt in her hand, her eyes blazing hatred as he walked toward her. "It's all over," he said as he halted alongside the horse. "I'll take my gun." Alicia leaned forward in the saddle, reached her arm out with the gun when she suddenly flicked her wrist, surprising quickness fed by desperation.

The heavy Colt slammed into his forehead, almost between his eyes, and he felt the pain explode through his head as he staggered backward. He went down as his legs gave out under him and he shook his head to fight away the blurred vision that dropped over his eyes. His sight cleared enough for him to see Alicia charging the horse at him. He saw the animal's hooves coming at him as his vision blurred again, but he flung himself sideways. The heavy pounding of horseshoed hooves shook the ground alongside his temple as he rolled again, and his vision cleared as he pushed to his feet. Alicia faced him, moving the horse toward him, and he backed until something told him to glance behind him. With a curse, he saw he was only a few feet from the edge of the drop-off.

He halted, started to move left, and Alicia moved the horse with him. She did the same as he moved right, each time moving closer. A smile of icy triumph had come to her full lips and he saw she still held the Colt in her hand. He started forward, directly toward her and she brought the horse up on its hind legs, forefeet waving in the air, ready to crash down on him. Fargo halted, drew back, and she brought the horse's forelegs down. But she continued to move closer and Fargo realized he was running out of room.

He realized something else: she didn't have to hit him with the gun, she didn't have to close with him. All she needed was to smash into him with the side of the horse. The animal's weight and power would do the rest. He'd be sent flying over the edge that was now so terribly close. He halted, crouched, his every muscle tightened as he watched her eyes. The icy smile stayed on Alicia's face as he saw her wrists move, a slight pull on the reins. The horse responded and started toward him at an angle where she could slam the animal's side or rump into him. His eyes narrowed as he watched her; he caught the faint movement of her wrists again and then her heels digging into the horse's side.

Fargo was ready as the horse charged forward and then swung around at Alicia's bidding. The horse's rump brushed against him, but only a grazing blow as he leapt in the same direction. He reached out, tried to seize Alicia's leg, but she swung the horse and he had to twist away to avoid being struck full by the animal's powerful rump. Alicia turned again, quickly and tightly, giving him neither time nor room to get away from the edge of the drop. She was coming at him again, from the other direction this time. Sooner or later one of her swipes would strike, he knew, and it would be over. He wouldn't wait for the inevitable. He'd make the moment come his way, take the gamble before it was too late.

He half-crouched again, his eyes on Alicia's wrists as she edged the horse toward him. Watching her wrists gave him that extra split second of time that would be lost if he watched her eyes. He was ready again as he saw her wrists tighten, turn downward ever so slightly. The horse responded, swerved its side toward him. Alicia expected him to run in the same direction again, repeat the same countermove he had done last time. She had adjusted for it, he saw with grudging admiration, and lengthened the angle as she sent the horse at him.

Fargo started forward, dug his heels into the ground, and halted; he twisted his body and dived under the horse's belly. He felt the horse's hind legs slam into him. But he had expected that, kept his body relaxed, and the collision sent him flying sideways instead of rupturing tightened muscles. He hit the ground on the other side of the horse, grunted in pain, but leapt to his feet to see Alicia reining to a halt in surprise. She tried to turn the horse, but Fargo was leaping at her, his arm wrapping around her leg to yank her from the saddle.

She kicked out, twisted her body away, and he felt her leg pull from his grip. He saw her disappear from the saddle as she fell from the other side of the horse. He raced around the rear side of the animal just as Alicia landed. She hit the ground right at the edge of the drop-off, half-turned to see him coming at her. She tried to roll as she leapt to her feet, and Fargo saw the edge of earth give way. His shout of alarm was pure reaction, and valueless as Alicia went over the edge. He half-turned away as he heard her scream, and he skidded to a halt. Her scream rose up, a long, wailing sound that came to an abrupt end.

He drew a deep breath as he stepped to the edge of the drop and peered down. Alicia lay crumpled on top of the rocks at the bottom of the drop. She looked all for the world like a discarded doll tossed away. Perhaps no worse than a hangman's noose. he reflected as he turned away. He saw his Colt on the ground where it had fallen, picked it up, and reloaded as he walked from the edge. The force of habit asserting itself, he realized. He retrieved the throwing knife, wiped it clean, and finally climbed onto the Ovaro.

He rode slowly. There was no need for anything else. The time for hurrying was over. He let his thoughts go back to everything that had happened. There were still a few gaps, but he was confident he could close them before he went on his way.

The day was still full when he came in sight of Ellen's place. She was outside, racing across the front yard toward him before he came to a halt.

9

Ellen clung to him for a long moment and he felt her trembling. Her lips found his, pressed, finally pulled away. "You're alive. You've come back," she murmured.

"Had a few unexpected moments," he said, a mixture of ruefulness and relief in his voice.

"Who was it?" Ellen asked. "Who came to meet you?"

"Alicia," Fargo said, and watched Ellen's mouth fall open. She stared at him, disbelief in her eyes.

"No. Oh, my God, no," she breathed.

"From the start," Fargo said. "She planned every step of it. I was sure of it before I went. I just wanted that final proof."

"Where is she?" Ellen asked, and he told her all that had happened. She was clinging to him again when he finished. "I hated her. I knew she was unfaithful, greedy, mean-spirited, selfish. I never realized she was a monster," Ellen said.

"Maybe your father did, finally," Fargo said as he closed one of the last gaps. "Maybe he found how unfaithful she'd been to him. That's when he left everything to you."

"I wish he hadn't," Ellen said. "He was killed for

it." Fargo shrugged, unable to disagree. "And she never found the will. After all that, she couldn't find it. Maybe it'll never be found now."

Fargo glanced up at the day and saw it slipping into dusk. "I'm going to pay a visit to the bar in town," he said. "I used it to light the fires. It's only right I put them out there."

"Come back afterward?" Ellen said.

"Count on it," he answered, and her lips clung for a moment more before he returned to the saddle.

Night had come when he reached Clay Springs and the bar was growing crowded as he entered. He saw the bartender find him at once, his eyes full of questions. Fargo strode to the bar and glanced at Goldie at the end atop her stool. He thought he detected curiosity alter the usual impassiveness of her expression.

"Some of the boys took bets," the bartender said.

"You all lost," Fargo said, and the saloon fell silent at his words and stayed that way till he finished telling his story. The murmur of voices that rose then held subdued shock in it.

"On the house," the bartender said as he poured a bourbon.

"Fair enough," Fargo said as he drained the drink. The warm, bracing liquid felt good. The first good thing he had felt since the day began. Except for Ellen's lips, a reminder it was time to leave. He tossed a nod at Goldie and almost received a smile back as he strode from the saloon. He rode from Clay Springs into Ellen's arms. Her passions were carried to new heights, all the turbulent emotions let loose in the circle of the bed. When she finally lay beside him, her skin shone with perspiration and she slept, drained and satiated, and yesterdays consumed in the embers of passion.

He slept beside her until the sun brought the new day and they breakfasted in silence. All that had happened returned to Ellen with remembered pain and pleasure. "Get your horse," he said when the plates were cleaned and put away, and she obeyed without questions. She rode beside him as he led the way into the southern part of the Smokey Hills and she realized where he was going. "You're a good man, Fargo. This is nice of you," she said.

"What is?" he asked.

"Coming up here to tell Amos," she said, and he nodded. He reached the hillside where Amos Dillon had his hidden home and he slowed to a halt and waited. The wait was short as Amos pushed his way from the trees, a leather sack over one shoulder. He climbed down to where Ellen waited beside Fargo, his eyes going from her to the big man on the Ovaro.

"It's done, Amos," Fargo said, adding details that were needed to complete the picture. "Except for one thing," he added when he finished. Amos met his eyes, his weathered face expressionless, and Fargo saw Ellen frown at him. "The will, Amos," Fargo said. "Tom Johnson gave you the will."

He heard Ellen's gasp of surprise as his eyes stayed on the old recluse. Amos shrugged and allowed what passed for a smile, reached into the leather sack, and pulled out the roll of parchment. He handed it to Ellen. "I'd have brought it to you in time," he said. "When I felt it was safe."

"Amos means when he was convinced I could be trusted." Fargo smiled.

Amos Dillon's shrug was both honest and an admission.

"Thank you, Amos," Ellen said as she took the will

and put it into her saddlebag. "May I come visit you the way Daddy used to do?"

"I'd like that," Amos said, and turned away without another word. He climbed without looking back and disappeared into the trees.

Fargo and Ellen rode down through the hills and the day was nearing an end when they returned to her place.

"I'll be moving back to the ranch tomorrow," she said. "Daddy would want me to carry on."

"I'm sure he would."

"Will you stay on and run it with me, Fargo?"

"Sorry, honey."

"I'll give you this place. It'll be yours, to do whatever you want with. Will you stay, then?" she asked.

"Sorry."

"I'll make you a partner in the ranch. Will you stay, then?"

"Sorry, honey."

"Will you stay and make love to me every day for as long as you like?"

"Now you're talking," Fargo said.

Ellen gave a contented little sigh as she began to unbutton her blouse.

LOOKING FORWARD!

**The following is the opening
section from the next novel in the exciting
Trailsman series from Signet:**

THE TRAILSMAN #117
GUN VALLEY

*Fall, 1860, in Arizona Territory,
where a band of killers left a trail
of human blood until they met the devil
himself in a place called Gun Valley . . .*

The big man astride the magnificent black-and-white
pinto stallion weaved among gnarled, stunted junipers
that grew so thickly he couldn't see over or through
them. He had been immersed in this green maze since
seven o'clock this morning. But he wasn't lost. A
Trailsman doesn't get lost. Temporarily trapped, like
now, yes, but never lost. The sun guided him by day,
the stars by night, whether he was in the mountains of
Colorado, which lay behind him, or the vast semiarid
desert of the New Mexico Territory, which he now rode
across.

Occasionally, Skye Fargo glanced at the late-October
sun to get his bearings. In the absence of any landmarks
or a navigator's sextant—which he wouldn't know how
to use even if he had one—he had to rely on his dead-

reckoning abilities to reach his immediate destination. He estimated Tucson lay approximately 250 miles south by southwest. The vast majority of that distance would be barren desert. The maze of junipers represented a mild annoyance when compared to that caldron.

Passing through overlapping branches, Fargo came to a wide ravine. He reined the Ovaro to a halt at the edge of it. In the middle of it were shod hoofprints. He counted five sets. One of the horses had thrown its hind left shoe. The Trailsman did not need to dismount and make a closer inspection of the hoofprints to know the riders headed down the winding ravine at a trot less than two hours ago.

Looking up the draw, Fargo saw where they had entered it. He grinned and shook his head. It was obvious to him the riders had run out of patience with bothersome trees, the branches of which clutched and clawed like witches' gnarled fingers, and taken the path of least resistance in the ravine, regardless of where it led.

Fargo chose, however, to proceed on the course he had set. He rode down into the ravine. Crossing the hoofprints, he caught a whiff of smoke and immediately reined to a halt. Had the riders smelled the smoke also, he wondered, and gone to investigate its source? If they had, they were asking for trouble. This was Jicarilla Apache country. Under the very best of conditions, Jicarilla's were not the friendly sort.

The Apaches always camped near a source of water. The ravine unquestionably led to a stream. Some of the smoke rising from their cooking fires wafted its way up the meandering draw.

Sitting easy in his saddle, looking down the ravine, Skye Fargo had mixed emotions about what to do:

proceed on course, or detour to help the riders get out of a bad fix, if they hadn't already been killed?

He decided to go have a look. If the men had been slain, that would be the end of it. If there were signs of one or more being alive, he would figure out a way to rescue them.

Fargo reined the stallion to follow the hoofprints, then set him to lope. Rounding a soft bend, he saw a thin layer of smoke coming toward him and took to the trees, where he continued to follow the ravine.

After riding a short distance his wild-creature hearing picked up wailing of the type Indian females make over the loss of a loved one. Frowning, he began to slowly raise his gaze and stopped when he saw black smoke through the juniper's branches. He was close to the Apache campsite. Damn close.

He proceeded with caution and came to a bluff. He eased from his saddle and left the pinto hidden in the junipers while he crawled out on top of the barren bluff to survey things. The ravine did, indeed, lead to water. Torrents of run-offs had carved a deep gully that sliced down the bluff to combine with many other runoffs to create what Fargo knew was a surging, muddy turbulence, now reduced by absorption, then evaporation, to a mere trickle. Another bluff rose well beyond the stream. It was higher than the one on which Fargo lay.

Twelve wickiups stood a short distance above the high-water mark on the near side of the tiny stream. Jicarilla women stood or sat and wailed while they watched the temporary shelters burn. Two of the women clutched naked children to their bosoms. Three sat and rocked back and forth. They were covered with blood of the Jicarilla men whose butchered bodies they clutched. Five females lay faceup, their dead eyes staring at the sun. All five were naked. Even from his lofty perch Fargo's keen vision allowed him to see that their throats had been cut.

He didn't see any ponies or horses, not one live Jicarilla male, nor any of the white men, dead or alive. But he knew they had been there and done this. The Trailsman had seen these same trappings left by the same kind of no-good white men many times before.

Fargo stood to scan as much of the landscape as he could, mostly up and down the width and length of the barren expanse between the bluffs. He hoped to see the Jicarilla had caught and killed the five men, but he saw only the thin ribbon of water that glistened silverish in the bright sun's rays. Bends at each end of the bluffs, which ran east to west, denied him further eye-search.

Walking to his horse, Fargo reckoned the butchers had arrived at the encampment at a time when all but three of the Jicarilla men were away on a hunt. The absence of ponies suggested there weren't enough for those three, so they had been left behind to protect the women. In all probability he would find all three to be older men. He mounted up, entered the ravine, and followed the shod hoofprints down to the wickiups.

When one of the women spotted him, she alerted the others. They immediately ceased wailing and stood to watch him ride in. Their studious gazes didn't last long, though. They grabbed sticks and stones, then ran to engage the big white man. Fargo fended off the stones, grabbed the fast-moving sticks, and yanked them from the women's hands. He broke them in two and flung the pieces away.

Now the enraged females began to try pulling him from the saddle. Fargo did not know one word of the

Jicarilla dialect, so he resorted to sign language. He reined the Ovaro to follow a tight circle to keep the women off him while he signed, "I am not here to hurt you, I came to help you."

While their tempers remained the same, they did back off. Fargo stopped the stallion from circling. He raised both hands to show neither held a weapon, that he came in peace, then signed, "Where are your men?"

The women exchanged nervous glances, then talked it over. Finally, the eldest woman took a step closer to Fargo and signed, "Hunting."

That was what he had thought. He nodded to show he understood her sign, then asked, "How many hunt? In which direction did they go?"

She answered, "Fifteen," then pointed toward the east bend.

He noticed there weren't any young boys around, only girls too young to rape. He believed the boys had gone with the men, a common practice among most other tribes. He inquired, anyhow.

She told him six boys accompanied their fathers.

"Fifteen altogether, or twenty-one?" Fargo signed.

"Twenty-one," she signed back.

Now Fargo knew the strength of the Jicarillas, in case he encountered them. He then asked, "Is there anything I can do to help?" He doubted if there was, but he asked anyway.

She told him no. They were going to leave everything as is for the men to see when they returned.

Fargo nodded, then rode among the smoldering wickiups and all around the encampment to find whether or not the three dead men were armed with rifles or carbines, and to spot in which direction the shod hoofprints went when the men left. He saw two broken bows and several arrows, but no guns of any kind. The white butchers had also headed toward the east bend.

He rode back to the women, dismounted, and got the sticks of licorice he'd been saving for just such an occasion out of his saddlebags. He twisted them in half and gave a piece to each youngster and woman. They just stared at the black sticks. Fargo had to put a piece in his mouth and start chewing and sucking on it to show them how. He returned to his saddle and headed for the ravine. Looking behind, he saw them standing there, chewing on the licorice, their chins dripping wet with the black juice.

"How strange," Fargo muttered thoughtfully. What a big difference a little licorice can make, he mused. The settlers going west, the army soldiers, and Washington . . . especially Washington, have been going about it in the wrong way. They should try licorice sticks instead of bullets.

He glanced toward the east bend. Either the Jicarilla had killed the bastards, or they had not. In a way Fargo hoped they had not. He wanted to punish the dogs. But he knew that was a very remote possibility. They had headed east on clear, level ground. Chances were good he'd never run across them again. If he did, there would be hell to pay. At least they had put the junipers behind, something he still had to suffer a tad longer.

Fargo cleared his mind of all thoughts about the white men and concentrated on putting as much distance between himself and the wickiups as fast as possible. He didn't like the thought of tangling with that many Jicarilla men. When they returned and saw the brutal atrocities committed by the whites, no amount of licorice could bank their fires of hatred.

They will come looking for me to take their revenge

out on, he told himself, not the butchers, because I'm closer. Fargo rode up the ravine and left it when he got to place where he found the shod hoofprints that he now wished he'd never seen. Moments later he was wandering again in the green maze.

An hour before sunset he broke out of the juniper's tree line, which ended on a ridge that overlooked a broad area of flat terrain populated by stone monoliths only. While the view was breathtaking, especially with a lowering sun to lengthen the huge boulders' dark shadows, he refused to tarry and look. Normally, Fargo would, but not now. He remained concerned that the Jicarilla, whom he knew were excellent trackers, were closing in on him. In open country, like that he viewed from the ridge, they would never catch his powerful stallion. In order to lose the Indians he would ride until darkness came and swallowed him up. Fargo found a route off the ridge to the enormous stones below.

Passing among the monstrous boulders—several towered unbelievably high—he saw most stood perfectly balanced on single pedestals of smaller stones. He reckoned if he touched one of the brutes it would topple. Millennia of winds and rains, and all they carried, had polished the monoliths and their dainty pedestals as smooth as glass, and wherever the wind and rain had found a soft spot on the great boulders, they sculpted out that soft spot to leave interesting, if not remarkably beautiful, designs. While most were smooth indentations—much like navels—some were tunnel-shaped and went completely through the massive stone.

Fargo's preoccupation with the stately boulders was such that he didn't sense the Jicarilla's presence until it was too late for him to take evasive action. They swarmed from the shadows behind or leapt from atop the sunstruck gaint boulders and caught Fargo by surprise. He didn't want to add to their existing misery, but he had no other choice. Twisting and turning the Ovaro, he drew his Colt and shot the nearest three Jicarilla in the leg at point-blank range. Then he dug his heels into the pinto's flanks. The stallion charged out of the forest of stone sentinels.

And ran smack-dab into the young boys. They stood in a line facing him, with their bows and arrows poised to shoot. There was no way the Trailsman would shoot a youngster, even when faced with this life-threatening situation. So he held his fire, took his chances, and plowed through their line. Arrows flew past him going away. He set the Ovaro in a dead run and rode hell-bent for leather to put as much distance between him and the youngsters as he could before any could let another arrow fly.

He looked over his shoulder. Screaming, a pony-mounted Jicarilla broke out of great rocks. A dense cloud of dust churned in the ponies' wake. The young boys parted and ran to their ponies. The thundering pack of Indian ponies raced the gap they left. Fargo looked ahead. He wasn't out of the woods yet.

He reloaded the Colt. Holstering it, he leaned low over the Ovaro's neck and glanced west. The bottom of the huge, fiery red-orange sun appeared to melt and flatten where it touched the horizon. Darkness would come slowly.

An arrow shot past him. Then another. He glanced behind. The leader of the pack and the rider trailing him by half a length were staying up with the Ovaro. They trailed in his dust by about six lengths. Four Jicarilla had given up the chase. The boys lagged far behind. The race continued at a fast pace. Fargo glanced behind occasionally. At twilight it was down to the Ovaro and the two hard-running Indian ponies, and they were sticking with him.

As twilight rapidly faded, giving way to darkness, Fargo came to a rock-strewn area that he couldn't avoid. He wouldn't risk crippling his horse no matter what, and it was getting dark fast. He had two options: halt and shoot them, or proceed with caution. He decided to go with the latter, but keep the other option open. Fargo slowed when he entered the area. Colt in hand, he looked over his shoulder.

The Jicarilla had divided, but not slowed. Fargo knew their strong thirst for vengeance made them take chances. If he were them, he would do the same thing. Ponies could be replaced; an opportunity to kill, like this one, came only once. And that opportunity would soon be lost forever due to darkness. They matched the Ovaro's pace as they rode on his quarters, each no more than ten yards away, with their arrows aimed at him.

Reluctantly, Fargo twisted and shot to wound the man on his right. The bullet hit his upper left arm and knocked him off the pony. Before Fargo could swing around and shoot the fallen man's companion, he heard his bowstring twang.

The arrow plunged into Fargo's back, slightly above the left shoulder blade. His pain was immediate. He fell forward onto the stallion's neck and fired blindly at the bowman. Concurrent with the third shot he heard the man yelp. He looked in time to see him fall from the pony, then watched him tumble on the ground. Fargo hoped he hadn't killed the fellow. Fargo rode on.

Darkness came. Fargo believed he had finally shaken the Jicarilla. He reined the Ovaro to a halt, eased from his saddle, and felt along the arrow's shaft. He knew the point was embedded too deeply to pull it out. But it had to come out, otherwise infection was a certainty.

Gritting his teeth, he reached around and gripped the shaft. When he did, the point moved and searing pain instantly shot outward, all across his back, the left shoulder, the left side of his neck, and down his left arm. Perspiration appeared on his brow. "It's now or never," Fargo grunted. He took a deep breath and shoved.

The brittle shaft broke in two, where it entered his shoulder. Fargo held the fletched end to his face, but he vaguely saw the feathers, because he was staring blankly into the night, wondering, wondering . . .

Two days later the area all around the crusted hole in Fargo's back had swelled and become inflamed. He rode on parched earth now, heavily cracked and bone-dry. He thirsted for rain. Oh, how he longed for it. Only rain could soothe the pain that gnawed on his back and shoulder. Only rain could give him and the Ovaro some relief from the baking sun. Only rain could provide his faithful stallion with his fill of water. As the Ovaro relentlessly plodded across the sunbaked earth, his and Fargo's head drooped, and Fargo prayed for rain.

The next day the big man watched through blurred vision dark thunderheads build in the west. It looked as though his prayers were going to be answered.

By midafternoon the thunderheads had collected and the air become deathly still. Fargo's lake-blue eyes burned. His chiseled-face grew hotter by the moment. His mouth and raspy throat felt parched. His dry, hot lips were cracked. And he heard nothing but the blood in his temporal veins surging in cadence with every heartbeat. It sounded as though sand pumped in them. Fargo realized he was drifting into delirium.

At dusk his delirium was complete. His senses faded in and out. He was burning up with fever. "The arrow," he mumbled incoherently, "must come out." He collapsed forward onto the pinto's neck, his leaden arms hanged on either side.

Fargo vaguely remembered feeling the cool raindrops on his back, and the Ovaro halting at a pool of muddy water to drink his fill, and him slipping from the saddle and falling alongside the pool. It all happened in slow motion, as though in a distorted, fuzzy dream, without sound.

The downpour enlarged the pool to the point it spread onto Fargo's face. Coming out of his stuper, he rolled over and pressed up onto hands and knees, touched his lips to the muddy water, and swilled. Then he collapsed facedown and rolled out of the water. He lay there with his eyes closed and his brain swimming. Sick and weak, he tried to get up, but could not. His senses began to fade.

Before his hearing left him, Fargo heard men laughing. It sounded as though they were coming toward him, riding in a metal tunnel. He called out to them, and tried to rise again, and failed.

He lay on his side, stared through blurry vision, forgetting all that he heard. Boots broke into his swirling vision. He felt hands shake him and a whiskey voice that said, "He's alive, but only barely. What do you think, Boss? Kill him, or leave him to die?"

Boss answered, "Get his guns and horse, then leave him for the buzzards."

Numb, sluggish hands tried to prevent them from

taking his Colt, but a boot kicked them away. Fargo vaguely heard the Ovaro nicker a protest, the Boss shout, "Stand still, you purdy son of a bitch. I'm gonna get on you whether you like it or not."

The last thing Fargo remembered before his mind shut down was hearing the whiskey voice chuckle, then say, "Damn, Boss, you let that purdy horse git away."